Marble Grove

A Carin Trimble Mystery
Book One

––––––––

An Original Story By
R. C. Ducantlin

Original Cover Image By
Zamajk Cover Art
www.zamajk.com

eBook ISBN: 978-1-949211-85-6
Paperback ISBN: 979-8-858236-29-0
Hardback ISBN: 979-8-868028-21-2

Table of Contents

Prologue

Case ID :	A-111
Name of Deceased :	Marjory Ellen Mosen
Date of Report :	12-Apr-23
Cause of Death :	Gunshot wound to the chest.
Place of Death :	Glen Acres Nursing Home
Date of Death :	3-Apr-23
Time of Death :	Est. 02:00-04:00
Investigator :	Marcus Alvin Demchuk

Background

The victim lived at the Glen Acres Nursing Home for three years before her death. No immediate family to claim the body.

Details

1) No bullet fragments at the scene.
2) No staff or other residents heard the gunshot.
3) No exit wounds.

Shooter retrieved the bullet from the victim.
Method of bullet retrieval: Unknown.
People known to visit Marjory: None

Chapter One

"Cheat!"

"This man is not cheating you."

"Is he okay?"

"Yes, he'll be fine. Al, that is a fair price. Please relax, stand still, and stop waving your hands. You are making the nice man nervous."

"Cheat."

"Marcus Alvin, I want you to speak calmly and use your words." Mom places a hand on her son's shoulder, hoping he does not have a meltdown. Deena Demchuk is, as always, overdressed — fake pearls, red nails, and a maroon dress under a hairstyle imported from the fifties. The ensemble, makeup, and hairdo are the Midwest woman's preferred public appearance.

Today, like every other day, Deena chose a professional look for the expedition into the town center. Adding the pearls was required to accompany her son to a store and a business transaction. Nevertheless, the coddling mother insists she is wearing everyday clothes. Of course, she quickly tells anyone who gets it wrong that her name is pronounced Dee-nah.

"Mom, I know what they cost. Cheat."

"We talked about this and what would happen."

Al steps too quickly toward the glass counter, causing the shop owner to step back. Al points at the glass case.

"See right there. That is a 1985 Topps Kirby Puckett Hall Of Fame Rookie Baseball Card number 536. It is a lot of money."

"Sir, that card is rated *BGS Ten Pristine* and priced accordingly. Your cards are not rated. Some are particularly good. I might pay a certified collector to rate the best cards. Most of the others are in good to excellent condition."

"What does that mean?"

"Ma'am, it means the cards your son is trying to sell range from a couple of bucks to a few hundred. What I offered for the lot is a fair price.

"Cheat. I know what they cost." Rocking side-to-side and breathing too heavily for everyone's comfort, Al is losing it. Mom steps between Al and the counter to force her agitated son to look at her and avoid a meltdown.

"You know their value. Please, stop arguing and settle on a price that allows the nice comic book man to make money when he resells your comics and baseball cards."

* * *

Marble Grove, Minnesota, is the place people imagine when they hear the phrase Middle America. The classic Midwest town flourished in the early and mid-twentieth century. A township that had been fading from existence for a couple of decades before the renewal happened. The rural community was dying slowly, along with the elm trees perishing under the relentless Dutch elm disease. Local farms were closing or selling out to international conglomerates. Teens were graduating high school and migrating away to a better future. After beginning the replanting a dozen years ago, the young elms lining the streets and the town are beginning to grow again. The rural community's town council has invested in creating decent schools and a renewed downtown. A vibrance is returning to the rural community. The high school hockey team hasn't had a losing season in a decade.

The two-room mother-in-law residence the Demchuks parents built for their only child is at the back of their property, down the gentle hill. Not yet fully independent, the incident with the fork in the microwave was a setback for Al and his parents. Mom and Dad do not mind Al returning three times daily to the main house for meals.

Living independently is one thing. Terrible rainstorms, lightning, and thunder are another. Al maintains a bedroom in the house for those days he needs to be closer to the comfort he knew as a child.

Marcus Alvin Demchuk demands to be called Al, the same as his favorite uncle. The names his teachers and the other kids used are unacceptable — Marcus, Alvin, Marc, and Chukster will set off the kind man. Considered high-functioning on the Autism Spectrum Disorder (ASD) scale, Al is thirty and average in every way, including prematurely balding. Not easily seen, a vibrant personality lurks behind the round face of the working-class American. Except Al cannot hold a job for more than a few weeks.

On an ordinary Wednesday night, the son drops a bomb on his parents at the dinner table. Sitting on the same seat he has used his entire life, he waits for Mom to serve his tater tots before surprising his parents. Of course, Mom and

Dad wait for their son's ritual to complete. The placemat is centered, the knife placed left, and the fork and spoon right, all at a thumb's width from the edge of the placemat. The juice is at eleven o'clock and easily reachable. Finally ready, he gives his parents the news.

"I want to go on a road trip."

Giving Al a place to live independently reduced his social anxiety and gave him the confidence to live self-sufficiently. Al's ASD has not slowed his desire to become a well-rounded adult.

Where others see a handicap, John and Deena know a truth. The doting parents learned quickly that their son Al would exaggerate his disability to get his way. Using the wrong words, refusing to make eye contact, and insisting he is uncomfortable are all things Al will exaggerate when frustrated, annoyed, or not getting his way.

His parents will call it out when their son deliberately uses the wrong words and embellishes his mannerisms to keep people off-guard. Much to her annoyance, Dad is more apt than Mom to correct Al.

"A road trip Al? Are you sure?"

Deena raising her voice from the kitchen to ask a question grates on John. As always, he lets it slide. John lets a lot of frustration pass unquestioned. The gentle man knows two things about his life. One, Deena is not going to change. Also, a steady diet of *Columbo* reruns and several versions of *CSI* gave his son a love of a good detective mystery. A wannabe investigator, Al spends his time scouring the internet for cases to solve. A member of several sleuth forums, he enjoys the anonymous banter the digital world provides. His favorite is the *Find the Slayer* forum. The *FTS* forum administrators keep the conversations civil and focused on solving cold cases.

"Al, your mother had a question."

Al immediately becomes fidgety and nervous, causing a tater tot to roll across the table. After helping Al retrieve a wayward shredded spud, John lets his son's non-response slide and gives Deena a steely-eyed glare.

However intelligent they know their son to be, John and Deena are shocked that Al wants to take a road trip.

Hints from the forum and finding a pattern in nursing home deaths, the amateur detective is convinced an active serial killer is working in Hemingway County, Minnesota, and at least two of the surrounding counties. Al knows he must do something, yet he does not know whom to contact. The recently retired county detective, Kendel Oensted, ignored the amateur sleuth. A chain smoker for fifty years, COPD and failing eyesight forced the near octogenarian into retirement. Al has a hope — maybe the new detective will listen. Perhaps, with Al's help, the new detective can stop the next murder before it happens.

After selling his beloved baseball card and comic collections, Al drained his savings to buy a car. The car is a tool Al needs to solve the murders. John and Deena thought the car was a step in Al's slow growth toward an independent life. Al had shocked them when they heard why he bought the car.

"Where are you going to go on your road trip?" Perking

up at his father's question and more tater tots from his mom, Al is almost pleasant.

"I am going to the place where people connected the murders."

John realizes Al will visit locations where he thinks the serial killer has murdered people. John and Deena realize Al is serious and cannot talk their son out of venturing beyond Marble Grove. It required four tries for Al to pass his driving test. John kept working with his son until they both had confidence in his driving ability. During his road trip, his parents insist that Al call them frequently. They will also follow their son's movements through the credit card they gave him on his eighteenth birthday, the GPS in his phone, and the tracker Dad hid in Al's car.

Every morning, at precisely seven, after showering and brushing his teeth, Al ascends the backyard slope to the breakfast nook beside his mother's kitchen bench. Breakfast with his parents is the same every day. It never goes well when Mom wants to change things and give her men something different for breakfast or lunch. Nonetheless, knowing her son throws fits when someone attempts to change his habits, Mom tries every few weeks to introduce variety into the family's dietary routine.

"Good morning, Al."

"Good morning, Mom."

The fifties-idealized housewife, cooking apron and

bouffant included, today is another day Deena Demchuk spoils her family — especially her only son. Unfailingly, the attempted adjustments to her son's eating habits reveal Al's valid handicaps. Today is another attempt for Mom to try again to give her son something different for breakfast.

Deena and John watch their son perform the process he accomplishes every meal at the breakfast nook. Sliding into the bench side of the alcove, pushing the seat cushion awry, Al reaches under his behind and pulls the worn pillow back across the bench. After adjusting the location of his placemat, plate, cutlery, and glass of orange juice, Al is ready. Almost.

"This is not porridge and bacon."

Deena knows Al is in a mood. She tries to work past the angst in her adult son.

"You didn't comb your hair again. You have to remember to comb your hair. I know that this isn't oatmeal and bacon. It would help if you watched your weight. Less bacon is a good thing. It's made from eggs and is called an omelet. Drink your orange juice."

"Of course, I know what an omelet is. I want porridge. One piece of toast, two packets of oats, two bacon, and orange juice."

Mom shrugs at another failed attempt to alter Al's unchanging morning meal. She knows her son must follow a routine, and his food preferences are a non-starter for change. At least their son has grown out of literally stomping his feet and holding his breath. He learned skills from the clinic and takes pride in controlling his angst.

Knowing the ending before she tries, Momma Demchuk gently presses her son to alter his rituals.

"What if you're on the road one morning and the restaurant is out of oatmeal? They will make you an omelet or a bowl of cereal, or a waffle.

"Tomorrow is the first day."

"Yes, tomorrow is the first day of your trip. You can think of today, and the omelet, as a practice day. John, do you have anything to say?"

"Good morning, Al."

"Good morning, Dad."

"I meant to ask you, last week, how was it selling your cards and comics? Mom told me you argued with the buyer over price."

"He wanted to cheat me. I can pay the loan."

"I don't think he wanted to cheat you. He probably tried to get them at a lower price to make more money when he sells them. You can keep the money we loaned you for the car."

"Thank you. I knew what they cost."

"You mean you knew the market value of the comics and baseball cards. How did you know?"

"I found them on-the-line."

John ignores his son's phrasing. There is no need to try and change that which will not change.

"You researched the value of the comics and baseball cards online before taking them to the comic bookstore? Knowing their value before negotiating is smart. Mom told me you got a good deal on the car. I checked it out — it looks like a winner."

"A good deal. Yes. Duck says the car is good."

Dad knows some of his son's word choices begin as mistakes or attempts at humor. If Al uses the wrong word enough, it becomes his standard speech. Dad lets the error slide without correction and presses his son for information, emphasizing the correct name.

"You spoke to *Duke*, our mechanic?"

"A good deal. Yes. Duck says the car is good."

"We've talked about this." Even mild and kind John has limits.

"You know his name is *Duke*. Please don't call him Duck. It is disrespectful not to use the correct name for people. If Duke says it's good, then it's a good car. I went online and added you to our insurance. Al, I know you're a good driver. You've never driven far on your own. Do you think it's a good idea for you to leave Marble Grove?"

"Day trips are safe."

"*Day trips*. Where did you learn that phrase?"

"On-the-line."

"Online? Where online? Son, help me understand your plan."

"I looked at trip planners on-the-line. The maps on-the-line in my phone tell me which turns to take."

"Ah, that's why you insisted we upgrade your phone and buy the dash mount. You want the new technology for the maps. You're an adult, making your own decisions. These are big decisions. You know your plan to visit the places you found on the internet makes your mother nervous. Are you sure you want to do something like drive across the county when everyone will worry?"

Al looks down. Dad knows his son is thinking about making his mother nervous.

"I know."

No one, including Al, wants an anxious or upset Deena Demchuk.

"Why don't you try the omelet and tell me about your research? How is the detective work progressing? What did you learn?"

Waiting for the microwave to ding, Mom watches from the kitchen as Al bites into the omelet, sips juice, and answers his father's question. Deena knows her son is mimicking his father, eating the eggs and ham. Internally seething, she cannot accept that John understands their son better than she does. Waiting for the damn beep taking too long is adding to Mom's simmering anger. Al is oblivious to the tension.

"The last victim lived where Grandma died."

"You mean the hospital?"

"No, Dad, not the hospital. Grandma died at the home where old people live."

"Do you remember your grandmother? She died when you were six."

"I was eight, and I remember. An American Goldfinch nested outside the window. Grandma's room smelled like the blue stuff Mom uses to clean the windows."

The beep turns John's head, and he frowns at Deena, who is, again, rolling over and giving in to her son's wishes.

Instead of waiting and letting Al eat the omelet, Mom sets a bowl of oatmeal in front of her only child. Taking back the half-eaten omelet, without checking if Dad wants the eggs, true to her tart nature, she wordlessly dumps the breakfast into the trash. Dad looks back to his son, accepting his life as the conversational middleman in their household trio. Dad keeps his thoughts to himself and waits for Mom to step into the kitchen before asking.

"What about your detective work? What did you learn? Why are you taking this trip?"

"I know who is killing the people. Shot in the heart."

"How can you know? How can you be sure? Do you have proof?"

"No proof. I know. All the people who were killed were going to die soon. The killer ended their suffering. Shooting someone in the heart is not a simple way to kill someone."

"Did you learn about suffering online? Did someone say those words online in your groups?"

"Yes."

Al's matter-of-fact tone about death is no longer worrisome to his parents. They chalk up his attitude toward death and use of tart detective language to too many crime dramas and amateur sleuth forums. Fortunately, they stopped a burgeoning habit of obsessively quoting crime dramas.

"Why shoot them in the heart? How many have been shot in the heart? Is the information you collected something we should take to your Uncle Al?"

"I don't know how many." Al's tone changes and it is a

clue that tells John that his son is becoming frustrated.

"Al, I trust you. If you have learned something important, maybe we should call Uncle Al."

"Too many. No proof."

Dad knows his son too well. After thirty years of observing and learning, Dad understands Al's speech and word choices are beginning to become staccato. Although his son's command of English is outstanding, the wannabe detective uses incorrect words and phrasing when he feels frustrated or anxious. Al's speech reverts to one or two-word responses when annoyed or nervous, a habit his parents have been unable to correct.

"Son, look at me. Who do you think is killing the people you found online?"

"A doctor is killing terminated cancer patients."

"I think you mean terminal."

Mom mills around, spoiling her son and ignoring her husband. Al continues on and on about how he has solved the murders, refusing to accept his father's advice for outside help. Dad presses his son for details. Al does not have a name for the murderer, nor can he confirm the deaths are real and that the victims were murdered.

Chapter Two

Lauren Helphia Mancone, née Whitecloud, is called *Louie* by everyone except her mother. Of course, it would be too soon if Lauren never again heard *"Louie Louie"* by *The Kingsmen*. Raised by a single mother, Louie's earliest memories are dreams of a beautiful life beyond the Reservation. At 29, Louie is tall, with amber skin and coal-black hair that reaches her waist. She cringes every time someone gives her the compliment: *Louie, you should have been a model.*

After making her way out of the Reservation and into a community college, good grades led the ambitious woman to a state university. Better grades resulted in a grant for graduate school. The Reservation Elders' stipend meant she could replace ramen noodles with healthier pre-packaged meal options at graduate school.

As a physician assistant specializing in oncology, working full-time, and attending school at night, Louie is proud to have completed her education with a PhD in nursing. In addition to her full-time job at a prestigious medical facility, Louie finds time to give back. Two Saturdays every month, the PA is called "Doc Louie" and is the only care provider at the small clinic on the nearby Reservation. Accepted by the local tribe elders, Louie is an outsider to the Minnesota indigenous group. She was made a tribe member and is a welcome addition to the small native community.

Kelvin Bryan Mancone is Louie's husband of two years.

Kel works from home as a data scientist and application development lead. Also twenty-nine, the rail-thin computer nerd knows he is one lucky SOB. The couple met in college in a women's studies class. Kel took the elective course to meet girls. He knows he won the lottery when he met and soon married First Nation's Louie.

The couple dote on a four-year-old border collie Louie brought to the marriage. Called Booger, the dog loved Kel immediately. Kel is okay with being a close second to Booger for Louie's love.

Unlike the barren and dusty desert of her Southwestern homeland, for Louie, the young trees lining the idyllic streets of Marble Grove symbolize a renewed future for the town too tough to die. She has always known a life of struggle and basic survival. The trees are her touchstone for a better life, so much so that she memorized the information the town published about the replanting effort.

"We are happy to announce the ongoing investment in the future of Marble Grove, which includes planting disease-resistant elm varieties. The American Liberty Elm (Ulmus americana 'Liberty') and Princeton Elm (Ulmus americana 'Princeton') have been shown to possess a level of resistance to Dutch elm disease."

Marble Grove is the first place where she feels at home and does not feel like she is in a holding pattern, waiting for the next tragedy to arrive.

In her mind, the desert was a prison, and Marble Grove had become her freedom. Unlike the desert of her childhood, Louie prefers the upper Midwest and its abundant life. Older homes on the reservation were often ramshackle. Her home in middle America is old. Old does not mean shabby. The home is well-kept. Checking to ensure the new trees have not disappeared overnight, Louie is readying herself for work. Happily, she looks through windows without the security bars of her childhood.

Unhappy that Kelvin hasn't postponed another business trip, the compassionate PA is wary of starting another argument. Too many nights alone are not what Louie thought came with the 'I do.'

"Five days is too long for you to be away. Booger hates being locked up all day. Can't you cut it down to one day? One day means Boog has to spend less time alone."

"How do you figure?"

Pulling her hair tight and checking the mirror, Louie expected the question. What she wants is in the mirror — a long black ponytail tied with four scrunchies in a thin, tight bundle.

"When your meetings are three days, you leave on Monday afternoon and return on Friday morning. Booger is alone all-day Tuesday, Wednesday, and Thursday — three full days of being locked up until I get home from work."

Kel downs the dregs of his coffee and sighs. He knows this is a battle he cannot win. He can't change his business trip or his wife's mind.

"Come on. We've talked about this and why it's important to my career. Booger was alone while you worked before we got married. When the application's new release is published, I can cut back on the travel. The alpha and beta testing are complete. We're making the final adjustments to the interconnections and the interface. It should be ready for release in a few weeks. What's bugging you? Did something happen at work?" Kel gets nothing from Louie.

"Lauren? Are you upset with me?" Her head perks up at Kel not using Louie. His repeating her given name, Lauren, is a message.

"No, you know better than to ask that question. If I were upset with you, *you'd know*." The tart response rolls off Kel and reminds Louie of why she married him.

"Using Lauren worked. It got you to listen." Kel stands, moves closer to his wife, and waits for her to look at him. A sideways glance is enough. He asks.

"Did something happen at work?"

Gripping the dresser, breathing, and considering, Louie raises her head and turns to face the man she knows is trying to help.

"No. Yes. I mean, it's the same. The older patients are kind and happy to see us. The younger patients, not all, a lot of them, are terrible. You tell them to lose weight, eat better, and take a walk, and what do you get? Rudeness and willful ignorance. Middle-aged patients are the worst. Obesity. Type 2 diabetes. Hypertension. We try so hard to help them even though many refuse to accept that their lifestyle contributes to their health problems."

"And?"

She looks past Kel at the new trees, wondering if the

replanting effort will flourish. She knows the trees are a projection — will she flourish? With a deep sigh of acceptance of her husband's nature, his need to help, and wanting the conversation to end, Louie admits the cause of her frustration.

"The pain trial is not going well."

"Honey? What happened?"

Lifting her access/ID badge from the bowl on the dresser and draping the lanyard around her neck, Louie looks at the man she knows is trying hard to make her life happy.

"Kel, it's just another day."

"No, it's not. What happened? Please, explain it to me."

"Nothing. You can't solve everything. I have to go to work."

Booger senses the tension and brings over his leash, dropping it at Kel's feet. Reaching for the leash, Kel tries one more time to ease his wife's troubled mind.

"Lou?"

"Yes, Kel?"

"Whatever happened, it is not your fault."

"How can you know that?"

"Because you could never hurt anyone. Come on, Boog, let's go."

Car keys are in her hand, and while watching through the window, Louie sees her two loves turn onto the sidewalk. One day, the young trees will be mature, and the sidewalk will be shrouded in the shade of tall elms. Kel waving to the neighbor is the sign reminding Louie it is another workday. The PA takes a deep breath, sighs, and heads into another day of frustrating patients.

"Every day is the same. Maybe today will be different."

＊＊ ＊＊ ＊＊

Carin Marcia Trimble, the newly promoted Hemingway County detective, is thirty-four and unmarried. The brunette is stocky with bright eyes, a beautiful smile, and a couple of decades of martial arts training in her tool kit.

Raised on a remote ranch in the Texas panhandle, Carin's path from becoming a farmer's wife, living a life of desperation in a double-wide, was to join the Marines. Trained as a military policeman, Carin used the GI Bill for her degree in criminal justice. Honorably discharged, Carin was immediately hired as a patrol officer by the Marble Grove Hemingway County Department of Police, or MGHDP. Jointly funded by the town of Marble Grove and Hemingway County, the multi-jurisdictional police force operates under one chief of police. Myron Albert Johnston has been in the role for nearly nine years and is the first police chief in sixty years not named Zumbro or Kolston.

For eight years, patrol officer Trimble waited for the only detective the MGHPD ever knew to retire. The only detective within one hundred miles of Marble Grove annually rejected retirement. Carin did not receive the promotion until the doctors refused to sign off on Kendel Oensted's fitness report.

Pride in her promotion comes with a cost. Detective Carin has resigned herself to the idea she will live her life alone. Eligible partners in Hemingway County are few and far between. Also, she has decided men are a hassle, and women are worse. Living a simple life in a two-bedroom bungalow that was built in the thirties, Carin ignores the geographic social reality every morning.

The number one button on her microwave is cracked and missing a piece of plastic covering. Yet, she refuses to replace the microwave. Her unmanicured fingernail pushes the tiny, exposed switch.

Unvarying in her morning routine, she presses the broken button and two others to start a one-minute, thirty-seven-second countdown — enough time to heat the frozen breakfast and brush the knots out of her bedhead. Honoring her days in the desert, always a Marine, she uses the same folding hairbrush she kept in her kit.

The detective is happy with her life. Why change anything when everything is okay? What's a bit of missing plastic in the immense wonder of life?

Today's pre-packaged breakfast of too much sodium and fat is interrupted by the messaging app on her phone chirping with bird calls.

Arriving at the nursing home, Carin is surprised by the size of the building and the lack of cars in the lot. The empty lobby has the detective wondering.

"*What are the visiting hours? I hope friends and family visit in the afternoon.*"

Stepping up to the reception desk, a bored receptionist looks up, raises an eyebrow, and turns to see a woman walking up to the visitor.

"Hello, I am Detective Trimble."

"Come this way, Detective. I'm Xarta Williams. I'm the general manager here at Glen Acres. Your assistant is already here."

"I don't have an assistant." Carin's tone worries Xarta.

"He mentioned he was your assistant and requested to see the body. I took him back to the patient's room."

Carin races with Xarta to the room of former resident Marjory Ellen Mosen. The women find a squat man with a serious face standing to the side, near the window. Carin surveys the scene, finding the dresser is overflowing with family pictures. Looking at the body, humming, the man appears to be thinking. Two emergency medical technicians, the first responders, one male and one female, are on the opposite side of the bed. Everyone is looking at the man, listening to the humming, and waiting for the detective's instructions.

"Who are you?" Unnecessarily, Carin's police tone leaked out.

"There is a red-crested cardinal near here. Hear that? That is the song of a red-crested cardinal." Looking at the odd man, Carin assumes he is correct.

"I asked you a question." Carin's tone has not softened.

"I know. Detective Trimble, I am Marcus Alvin

Demchuk. Here is my report."

Al hands Carin the single-page report from a manila folder.

"Report? Who are you?"

"I am an investigator. Not officially. I know about the murders. I know who has been killing the people with the cancer."

Xarta steps forward to interject.

"I am sorry, Detective Trimble. I will call security."

Before Xarta can react, Carin recognizes Al's differences and adjusts her tone.

"No need, Mrs. Williams. I don't think Marcus is harmful."

"Alvin."

"I'm sorry. Alvin, did you touch anything in this room?"

"People call me Al."

Carin breathes, remembers her training, and reminds herself to be patient — and to use a pleasant tone.

"Al, did you touch anything in this room?"

"No."

"How did you know my name?"

"I did not touch anything. I saw you on the news."

"News?"

"Do you hear that? That is a monk parakeet. Escaped parrots are in twenty-three states. When you were promoted to detective, I saw you on the news."

Carin suspects Al is giving false information. With some research, she will confirm her suspicion — in

Minnesota, no known parakeets exist in the wild. She accepts the raised eyebrow from the female responder and a shrug from Xarta.

"Thank you for the information. I'll take over the investigation from here. Please follow Mrs. Williams back to the lobby. When I'm finished here, you and I can review the case. Is that okay?"

"Yes. I will wait in the lobby. Detective Carin Trimble. Marjory Ellen Mosen."

After waiting for Al to leave with Mrs. Williams, Carin leans in to check the gunshot wound.

"Have you two seen gunshot wounds?"

The male EMT shakes his head negatively and looks at his partner.

"I've seen too many GSWs." The female EMT has a crisp, professional tone.

"You've seen more than a few GSWs?"

With a sad tone, the female EMT shrugs and answers.

"I've been doing this a long time."

"What do you think?" Carin forces a smile with her question. The female EMT steps forward and amps up the professional attitude.

"Marjory Ellen Mosen, 81, gunshot wound to the chest. Small caliber weapon. Someone gave Marjory a gift."

"Gift?" The new detective is intrigued.

"If Marjory wasn't dead when she was shot, death was a gift. See that I-V? Marjory was on enough pain meds to stun a horse."

Standing tall as Mrs. Williams returns, Carin eyes the I-

V, then a red-colored bird on the windowsill.

"I am sorry, Detective. I will ensure the staff is trained on security procedures. For what it's worth, Marjory had stage-four mesothelioma."

"Mesothelioma?"

"A cancer in the lining of the lungs."

"Mrs. Williams, did anyone hear anything?"

"None of the staff heard anything unusual. Also, none of the guests mentioned hearing anything. Of course, the overnight staff is limited."

"Limited?"

"There are two on the overnight, an assistant and a receptionist. This facility has two hundred rooms. A couple of rooms turnover every month or so."

A stream of death in the facility has Carin wondering. Unlike the desert, she notices that the air handling that is cooling the building is delaying the odor of death. The room's thermostat confirms Carin's premise. The facility's policy is to turn down the air when someone passes.

"Let me guess. The overnight staff was asleep when it happened. The assistant and a receptionist found Mrs. Mosen this morning when she didn't turn up at breakfast."

Silence is Carin's confirmation. Xarta steps aside, permitting the MGHC forensics team to enter the room. Carin observes the first forensics person, a male, snapping photos while the second, a female, examines the body. Carin moves to the window as a second red bird lands on the sill.

While watching the birds flit around in a courtship

dance, she wonders why someone would kill a dying woman.

"Money? This place is not for people who have money. Spite? Who kills a little old lady out of spite? And then again, could it really be to put her out of her misery? Altruistic? Why risk everything for a stranger?"

The birds fly away. Exhaling, the detective wends her way back to the front and finds Al in the lobby.

"I need to see some identification." Regretting her tone, Carin pushes the remorse out of her mind.

Al hands over his state-issued identification card. Carin is aware of the man's hands moving unnaturally. Flittering as if looking for something to hold, Al presses his hands to his shirt to stop the movement. Then, holding out a hand, Carin quickly realizes Al expects the detective to provide him with her business card. Handing over her card, she watches Al closely.

"Al, are you nervous?"

"Yes."

"Don't be nervous. Nothing is going to happen to you. This ID says you live in Marble Grove. I live in Marble Grove. That is over an hour from here. How did you get here? Do you live here?"

"I live in Marble Grove. I drive. Here."

Accepting Al's driver's license, Carin realizes she has made Al's tics worse by questioning his ability to drive a car. The self-proclaimed investigator refuses to look at Carin.

"Oh. Sorry. Okay. Did you come here this morning?

Please, look at me." Guilt and remorse do not come quickly or easily to the detective.

"Yes." Al's short answers are unnerving. He looks up with his one-word reply, then quickly tilts his head down and returns to scanning the carpet.

"Yes? You came here this morning?"

"Yes."

"How did you know Mrs. Mosen was dead?"

"I figured it out."

"Figured what out? Murder. What are you talking about? I need you to help me understand."

"The serial killer. The doctor is killing terminated patients. I figured it out. I knew Marjory Ellen Mosen was next. I saw the dispatch." Al looks from the floor to the window and back to the floor, expecting the next question.

"Terminated? Do you mean terminal patients? Dispatch? Do you mean the call for the first responders? You are going to have to help me understand. What are you talking about?"

"The serial killer. A doctor is killing people with terminated cancer."

Al and Carin turn their heads to watch the first responders roll Mrs. Mosen's body through the lobby. Stopping and waiting for the sliding doors to open, the female EMT turns to Carin.

"Detective, I have seen a lot of GSWs. This one was up close and personal."

"Up close? How close? Are you sure?"

"I'm sure. Someone pressed the gun barrel to the chest

before discharging the round. The coroner will confirm. I know I'm right."

"Thank you..."

"Mari. Mari Cochran."

"Thank you, Mari."

Chapter Three

"You just got back and already have another trip planned for next week? That means you'll be away three weeks out of the last two months." Louie internally cringes at the sharp tone and vibe she is emitting. Kel deserves better.

"I told you. When the app is released, I'll cut back on the travel. The team is counting on me to get this project over the line."

Pulling her blouse over her head, hiding her lace bra, Louie knows she is becoming bitter. She knows it's not Kel's fault her attitude is becoming terse and irritated — yet.

"Damn it, Kelvin, you promised to change your schedule. Look at him. Booger knows you're packing again."

"I'll walk him before I head to the airport. It will be okay. Booger will be okay. We will be okay. Just a few more weeks, and then I'll walk Booger every day."

"Whatever. You gave me the same story last time."

"Are we talking about Booger being home alone, or are we talking about you?"

"We are talking about the dog. I'm a big girl and can take care of myself."

Kel winces at his wife's biting reply, then watches his love stride away, knowing he has to make a change.

"Hello, Detective Trimble."

"Hello, Mari. Hello. . . I'm sorry I didn't get your name the other day." Carin is pleased to see Mari and the male first responder she met at Glen Acres in Marjory Mosen's room. She is delighted at the encounter and muses.

"Why do these rooms smell musty with a hint of window cleaner?"

"Ashton Walker. Call me Ash. Detective Trimble, you're getting all the oddball cases. Are murders of old people in retirement homes your specialty?"

Ignoring the youngish first responder while admiring his smile and biceps, Carin wonders if Ash and Mari are a thing. Both are young, fit, and good-looking. Hours upon hours side-by-side in a response vehicle leads to interesting personal dynamics. Personal dynamics. Carin wants *personal dynamics* in her life. The detective refocuses, then turns from the dead woman lying in the bed to Mari.

She hadn't expected to see the response team again so soon. It's been a week, and here they are, in another room in a managed care facility.

"Okay, Ash. Mari, what do we have?"

"Mary-Ethel Smyth, seventy-seven. This is the same as Marjory Mosen. Mary-Ethel was shot in the heart."

"Shot? Another one? Here, in the nursing home?"

"They call it a long-term care facility. And yes, Mary-Ethel was shot." Carin grins because Ash's pedantic comment came with a stink eye from Mari.

"Mari, do you think Mary-Ethel was asleep or dead when she was killed?"

"I think she was asleep or waited quietly for her heart

to explode. You're the detective. You tell me."

"Forensics or the coroner will confirm how Mary-Ethel died. Are you sure she was shot? I don't see burn marks."

While leaning in for a closer look, Carin's semi-rhetorical question receives a response.

"Who runs this place?"

"I do."

Turning on her heel, Carin sees a thickset woman enter the room wearing a stained and oversized gray jumpsuit. Carin suppresses her military training. Gaining the respect of others begins with being clean and tidy at all times. It's called *Military Bearing*, and Carin thinks more people should live their lives with confidence in themselves and their abilities.

People need to learn bearing.

"And you are?"

"Thera Thompson. I'm the director of Golden Hills Care Center."

"Mrs. Thompson."

"It's Miss. Call me TeeTee."

"TeeTee, do you have access to the security recordings?"

"I do. There are no recordings."

"Let me guess, no money to fix the security system."

"I called the night crew. Burt and Chanell didn't see anything. Burt is the custodian and was probably asleep when it happened. Chanell's our front desk assistant and was likely asleep. There's not much going on after the cleaning is complete, and the end-of-day reports are wrapped and sent to corporate. It's a good overnight gig for people who need a second job."

Thera Thompson, aka TeeTee, forces a false smile, stretching the poorly applied makeup across her face. What used to be called Boot Camp, Military Basic Training, was easy for the eighteen-year-old Carin Trimble. She entered boot camp with a meticulous nature. The detective pushes aside her dislike for frumpy people before responding to the facility director with a tart question.

"Do all long-term care facilities have two overnight employees? Two that are allowed to sleep on the job?"

"They are not supposed to sleep. The call buzzers will wake them if needed. As far as I know, for a facility this size, two overnight staff is a standard business model in this industry. No one questions what the team does after the work is complete. Finding people with experience, who are willing to work the overnight shift, is not easy. Being flexible is necessary."

Pulling on her gloves, Carin leans in for a close look at the body.

"Mari, does this look like a gunshot wound to you?"

"Yes. A twenty-two or twenty-five caliber. Maybe a thirty-two. My money is on a twenty-two. Cheap and easy to get."

"No burn marks? Is that odd, Mari?"

"Kind of. Anything is possible. Ask forensics."

"Ash?"

"A twenty-two, up close, and very personal."

"You two seem knowledgeable on firearm damage. Is

there new training for EMTs in GSWs?"

Ash defers to Mari using a head tilt and an unconscious bicep flex.

"Yes, there is new training. AR-type wounds are treated differently because of the congealing effect on the internal organs. Small-caliber injuries are more straightforward. I didn't need the training. I learned to ID and treat GSWs in the Army. I was trained as a Combat Medic Specialist."

After eyeing Mari sideways, with evident respect, Carin is complimentary.

"Thank you for your service."

Director TeeTee uses Mari's silent acceptance of Carin's compliment to interrupt.

"Detective?"

"Yes?"

"You should know that Mary-Ethel had stage-four esophageal cancer. A week, maybe two, is all she had left."

TeeTee's walkie-talkie crackling grabs everyone's attention.

"Tee, there is someone in the lobby asking for a Detective Carin."

"Tawniqua, who did you say is in the lobby?"

"He says he is Detective Carin's assistant."

"We'll be right there."

Carin stares at the blood-soaked night shirt before issuing orders, then stepping around the arriving forensics duo and leaving the small room.

"Mari, you and Ash wait for forensics to finish, then clean this up. Before you leave, ensure I know how to contact you both. I may want to pick your brains."

On her way into the facility, Carin missed noticing the shabby and rundown lobby. Every other light fixture is dark.

"They are saving pennies. This facility is struggling financially."

Looking around, the man from the room a week ago is waiting near the dirty window.

"His name is Al."

"What are you doing here?"

"I brought you my report."

She doesn't reach for the report when Al holds it out.

"You are not a detective. It's Al, right?"

"Here is my report."

Al pushes the report toward Carin again.

"Did you drive over? Al, it's almost two hours from Marble Grove to here."

"I drove. That is a common house finch."

"What?"

"There, on my car — that yellow bird is a common house finch."

Al points through the sliding glass doors to his car, parked in one of the first spaces not designated for disabled people.

"The bird is nice. Why are you here?"

"It is a common house finch. I came so you have my report. I created the report."

"I understand. Al, you can't keep showing up at crime scenes. You could have emailed your report. In the future, please email them to me. Okay?"

"I have a report."

"Okay, give me the report. What do you want?"

"I don't want anything. See, I knew Mary-Ethel was going to be next."

TeeTee, watching Al and Carin's exchange, decides to step forward.

"Al, my niece is like you. She often helps me here at the facility. Are you trying to help Detective Trimble?"

Beaming and swaying with joy, Al's one-word response gives Carin a new understanding.

"Yes."

Chapter Four

Case ID :	A-112
Name of Deceased :	Mary-Ethel Smyth
Date of Report :	9-Jun-23
Cause of Death :	Gunshot wound to the chest.
Place of Death :	Golden Hills Care Center
Date of Death :	10-Jun-23
Time of Death :	Est. 02:00-04:00
Investigator :	Marcus Alvin Demchuk

Background

The victim lived at the Golden Hills Care Center for seven years before her death. Immediate family moved. No money for burial.

Details

1) No bullet fragments at the scene.
2) No staff or other residents heard the gunshot.
3) No exit wounds.

Shooter retrieved the bullet from the victim.
Method of bullet retrieval: Unknown.
People known to visit Mary-Ethel: None

Reading Al's report over Carin's shoulder, TeeTee is dumbfounded by the details and is unable to remain quiet.

"Al, many of the items in your report are guesses. When you created the report, you couldn't have known some of those things you included."

"It is right. Like the others. It is the same."

"You are guessing." TeeTee is becoming defensive about a murder on her watch. Interjecting, with a slight hand movement for the director to step back, Carin remains focused on Al.

"Good detectives don't guess. How do you know about the family and their inability to pay for a funeral?"

Al refuses to answer, forcing Carin to press.

"Al, Miss Thompson has a reasonable question. How do you know Mrs. Smyth's family cannot pay for a burial?"

Al refuses to answer, stepping closer to the window and looking for birds in the trees. Carin's mind is flying and hits upon a new idea.

"Al, this report is titled A-112. Do you have 112 reports?"

Al continues to look for birds while he answers Carin.

"No."

"How many reports do you have?"

"Twelve."

"You have reports for twelve murders?"

"Yes. See? There! The nest is way up."

"Yes, Al, I see the nest." Carin lied. Turning with a nod toward the other side of the room, Carin silently requests TeeTee to step away, waits for the director to move to the other side of the lobby, and then steps closer to Al. Using a soft voice that is direct from her interview training, she asks the odd man for information.

"Tell me about the reports you created."

Interrupted by a resident walking in, trailed by TeeTee,

the resident marches close and joins the circle. Dressed in threadbare cotton pajamas and an equally tattered floral housecoat, the woman appears to have just gotten out of bed. Carin, TeeTee, and Al wait for the woman to speak. Annoying everyone in the room, the resident remains silent. Carin's eyes plead with TeeTee for help.

"Detective, this is Bertie Young. She has the room next to Mary-Ethel. Bertie, do you want to say something?"

"The nice man helped Mary-Ethel."

"See? I told you. Detective Carin, it is the doctor." Al is almost jubilant.

"Hold on. Please be quiet, or I will insist you wait outside. Mrs. Young, what man helped Mary-Ethel?"

"I don't know. I was peeking through the door. I was awake. I saw the man in the hallway."

"You were awake. Do you know when you peeked through the door?"

"Yes, it was 3:12 when I woke."

Al is beaming and rocking side-to-side.

"I have to fix my report. Time of death, 3:12. Detective Carin, we must find the doctor."

"Please. Stay quiet. I will not ask again. You and I will talk about the investigation in a moment."

Al turns toward the window with his head in his phone.

"Mrs. Young, can you tell me anything about the man you saw in the hallway? Anything you can remember will help. Was he tall? Short? Heavy? Thin? Hair color?"

"About like you, I guess. Not too tall. Not too short. Not too fat or thin. Dark shoes, pants, and one of those hoodies pulled up. I didn't see a face."

"I understand. That is helpful information. How do you know the man was nice?"

"Because Mary-Ethel was in pain. Now, she has no pain. It is nice she has gone to a place with no pain."

"Are you sure it was a man?"

"Yes. You know, it could have been a woman. You never know what is happening with people these days."

Checking her sparse notes, Carin decides she has enough information for the moment.

"Thank you, Mrs. Young. Miss Thompson, I will talk to your night crew. Did you say Burt and Chanell?"

"That is correct. Their shift begins at eleven."

"Tell them to expect a call from me at 23:30."

"Twenty-three-thirty?"

"Sorry, I will call them at eleven-thirty tonight."

"I will tell them to expect your call."

"Al, let's chat."

With a nod to TeeTee, the director accepts Carin's request to collect Mrs. Young and step away. Carin sits near the window Al is using to view the birds.

"Please sit."

Al does not sit. He shuffles and continues looking through the smudges on the window. Carin's phone chimes a birdcall. Checking, she finds the arrival of an email. Looking down, a quick check of the sender and subject line leaves Carin mildly surprised.

"Did you send me an email? I told you to email me. How did you get my email address?"

"It is on your card. You gave me your card when Marjory Ellen Mosen was killed."

"Can you email your other reports to me?"

"I have email on-the-line. I can use on-the-line in my phone."

"You have email online. That's good. Please send your reports to me."

"I will send the report using the on-the-line email. Your phone is not a bird."

"Al, I don't understand."

"The sound your phone makes is not a bird. Someone created the sound to make a fake bird."

"Okay. I will find an authentic birdcall to use. Al, how did you know Mary-Ethel was the next victim?"

"I can't tell you. It is HIPPY."

"Hippy? Do you mean HIPAA-protected?"

"Yes. HIPPY-protected."

"Are you saying how you found the information is HIPAA-protected?"

"Yes."

"Look at me. Please. How did you get access to private medical records?"

"I can't tell you. It's HIPPY-protected."

Carin stands, raising her spine to full height, thinking and assessing. Falling on the training she received, a deep breath is needed to confirm her thoughts.

"Al is not a kid or a kook giving me made-up reports and emails about a serial killer. My new assistant *is a hacker — a good one."*

"I have a lifetime of experience in being and feeling different." Carin accepts Al's comment with a minor epiphany. The detective realizes that Al selectively uses his condition to his advantage.

"Please, relax. It is okay to look at me when we are chatting." She tries to get him to make eye contact.

"People say I stare."

"It's okay to look at me when we're talking. I'll tell you if you're making me uncomfortable. Do you know what? We can talk later. Al, go home. Send me the reports right away."

"Right away."

"Yes, please. Al, when you get home is fine. I want to read the reports tonight."

"Tonight. Okay."

Al is bouncing with joy at Detective Carin's request for his reports. Carin recognizes she uses his name often when speaking to the man who is trying to become something more. Repeating his name helps confirm her new assistant is focused and listening.

"Al, go now. Drive safely."

*   *   *
**   **   **

Ignoring the terrible list of unpronounceable ingredients in her pre-packaged breakfast, Carin tugs at the knots in her bedhead. She is brushing her hair and thinking. After reading Al's reports, the new detective accepts the data and that the amateur sleuth may be on to something.

Her new assistant has ideas about a serial killer. His reports are unusable in a courtroom. They are impractical legally and speculative by definition. Yet, they have traction in the detective's mind.

If the reports are accurate, and she can prove it, Carin realizes that Al's theory about a serial killer is her career path out of Middle America and into the big leagues of detective circles. The Feds might be interested in someone who convicted a serial murderer. The new bird chime on her phone gently tugs Carin out of her head and into the present.

Arriving at the Louise Almond Hospice Facility, Carin recognizes Al's car before she pulls to a stop. Hospice is the facility's primary function, with follow-on sales a secondary objective. It is not a coincidence that the hospice shares a parking lot with a funeral home and mortuary. Entering the lobby, Carin is not surprised to hear Al trying to talk his way into the facility.

Waving his arms, talking too loudly, and stepping toward and away from the counter, Al is animated. He is not being aggressive. The woman behind the reception counter is watching the scene with a dry smile.

"I am a journalist looking for background on a story I am writing about healthcare facilities that accommodate people on the ASD spectrum. Also, I am considering authoring an article on a series of recent deaths in long-term healthcare facilities. Did Mrs. Bretherton have a visitor on the day she died?"

"No." The receptionist's lips barely moved.

"Did cancer get her?"

"We can't tell you that. For whom did you say you work? Never mind, I'm going to have to ask you to leave."

Before Carin can react, two people step in and begin to forcibly escort Al from the facility. Quickly flashing her badge, Carin saves Al from the embarrassment of being kicked, literally, to the curb.

"Gentlemen, he's with me. I am Detective Carin Trimble. Who is in charge here?"

"I am." The small man watching the security men manhandle Al squeaked and stepped forward.

"Who are you?"

"Jared McKinnon. I own this facility."

Ignoring the creepy nature of McKinnon's well-worn black suit, twitchy eyes, pale skin, and greasy hair, Carin steps closer. A couple of inches taller than the oily man, Carin begins the inquiry.

"Is the McKinnon Funeral Home and Mortuary yours, too? A hospice next to a funeral home — that's convenient."

"Yes. My father renamed the hospice for my mother. Louise Almond was her maiden name. The body is this way."

Trailing McKinnon and looking over the short man with slippery hair, Carin shudders and ponders the revenue stream of a hospice and adjacent mortuary and funeral home. The financial contemplation is interrupted when Al pulls a sheet of paper from his backpack and then steps quickly forward to hand Carin his report. The detective glances at the paper before she puts a finger to her lips and hopes Al understands the universal signal to stay quiet.

Chapter Five

Case ID : *A-113*

Name of Deceased : *Candice Alice Bretherton*

Date of Report : *11-Jun-23*

Cause of Death : *Gunshot wound to the chest.*

Place of Death : *Louise Almond Hospice Facility*

Date of Death : *11-Jun-23*

Time of Death : *Est. 02:00-04:00*

Investigator : *Marcus Alvin Demchuk*

Background

The victim lived at the Louise Alcott Hospice Facility for three weeks before her death.

Details

1)

2)

3)

"Al, I want you to wait in the hall." He twitches at the order. Nevertheless, Al complies by standing in the doorway. The first thing Carin notices is Al's latest report contains far less speculation. Her self-appointed assistant took the criticism to heart and adjusted his methodology.

The scant information is Carin's confirmation that Al wants people to think he is not nearly as intelligent as he is. The second thing she notices is there is no blood on the body. Mrs. Bretherton has been cleaned and covered in new bed linens. Pulling on gloves, confirming the thermostat is cranked down, and leaning in, Carin pulls back the comforter. Pulling down the nightgown, she glares at the wound over Mrs. Bretherton's heart — a tiny hole with no blood or gunpowder residue.

"Mr. McKinnon, did Mrs. Bretherton have a visitor yesterday? Do you know when she died?"

"No."

"No, meaning no visitors or no, you don't know when she was killed?"

"No, and no. Her cancer was bad. Pancreatic. She had a couple of days at most. We see a lot of people with pancreatic cancer."

"The cancer didn't get her. Why did you clean the body?"

"We have a lot of people visiting and touring the facility."

"You altered a crime scene because you were worried about appearances. Who is Mrs. Bretherton's next of kin? What is their contact information?"

"We can't tell you that. I don't particularly appreciate where this is going. Do I need to call my attorney? For whom did you say you work?"

"I am a detective for the town of Marble Grove and Hemingway County, assigned to investigate the murder of

Mrs. Bretherton. You can call an attorney if you want. I don't care one bit about what you appreciate or don't appreciate. A warrant is a phone call away. Mr. McKinnon, what are you not telling me?" Carin remembers her training and counseling sessions. She remembers the counselors telling her, ordering her, to keep her voice even in tone and flow.

"How did you know she was murdered?"

Before she can respond to McKinnon, Mari and Ash lean in through the doorway. Waved forward by Carin, they slide sideways through the door, avoiding Al, who has to rub his nose at the invasion of Mari's perfume. Mari pushes Ash deeper into the corner, allowing the forensics team into the now too-small room.

Carin nods to Al, hoping he takes the hint to remain out of the room. Glancing at Al, who is stepping back and remains close enough to observe, Carin is smiling to herself.

'Al is far more intelligent than he displays.'

The detective turns her harsh police officer's voice on the hospice owner.

"Mr. McKinnon, I have you on conspiracy to murder. Hiding evidence is a felony. We can do this down at the station, or we can be civil about the discussion. Tell me, and the forensics team, what happened and why you cleaned the crime scene."

Jared McKinnon looks around at everyone looking back, waiting for him to admit what he did.

"We can't let word get out that one of our guests was murdered inside our facility. Detective, you have to understand how this will affect my business."

"I understand you take advantage of people and families who are suffering. I know that protecting your cash cow is vital to you. I am not going to arrest you. I am going to charge you. My advice is to get a lawyer. Now, get out of this room and let these people do their job. Mari, Ash, let the forensics team finish, then find me and tell me what you think."

"Al, come with me."

In the hall, leading Al out of the facility, Carin immediately regrets her tone. In the parking lot, beside Al's car, she watches the would-be detective look for birds. A softer style is needed.

"I have to remember the training and the sessions. What did the counselor say? Using a soothing voice will go a long way. "

"Thank you for the heads-up. McKinnon was trying to pass off the murder as a natural death. You called in the death. How did you know?"

"I have to correct the report."

"Okay, Al, correct the report and email it to me. How did you know Candice Bretherton was murdered?"

"Someone called 911. Then they called back and claimed it was a mistake."

"I think I understand. You are monitoring the police band radio and dispatch. How do you know about the dispatch calls? Wait. It was a week between the prior killings. Now, there are two murders in two days. Why? How did you know? What are you doing to gather the data for the reports? Please help me understand. Please connect the dots for me. I have a report due to my boss and need information."

"Candice Alice Bretherton was going to die. People come here to die. Why do people go to another place to die? Home. People should die at home. Die in the hospital."

"I don't know. I guess these places help people and their families with the pain of dying and the trauma that comes from losing a loved one. Al, how did you know?"

"There is a mountain bluebird, a male, near here. This is not the normal range for a mountain bluebird. The mountain bluebird is Idaho's and Nevada's state bird. People think it is a western bluebird. It is a mountain bluebird. The eastern bluebird is Missouri's and New York's state bird."

"Al, why are you not answering my question?"

"HIPPY."

Again, she has to accept that Al understands he is illegally gathering information. Nothing he provides can be used in court. However, Al's information can help her find the killer.

* * *
** ** **

The Hemingway County municipal building was the largest construction project in the County in over sixty years. Finished two years ago, the sprawling facility is home to the Marble Grove City Council, the Hemingway County Board of Supervisors, the Town Council, the Police

Department, a Forensics Division, the County Jail, and the Regional Morgue. When the quarry closed, and two hundred people had to look for non-existent jobs, the county defaulted into the area's largest employer.

Carin has picked up the habit of avoiding entering the building from the rear. Entering the building from the side or front, she doesn't have to read the directional sign leading to the morgue.

The former marine has seen enough and doesn't need to see more death. From her office to the morgue, walking through the long, shiny corridors, the former Marine MP feels the dread rising during the short walk.

"Marc, what's up? Why did you call me to come down here? You know I'm not fond of this place. Morgues are depressing. Sorry."

Marc Downsen, the coroner, ignores the comment, allowing the new detective to continue.

"She has been here for a few days. Did you find something with Bretherton?"

"Carin, you need to see something. I went back and looked at the reports for the list you sent to me. The murders span about two years. A few years ago, you were the deputy who responded first to two of the deaths. Nine were initially reported as natural deaths from cancer. Now we know they were murdered. Not all thirteen have a similar injury."

"I responded to a call about someone dying, twice, when I was a deputy? If you say so. Do you think all the names on the list were murders? Are you sure?" Carin knows she has used the skills she learned in counseling to block the memories of responding to calls with death.

"Yes, come with me."

Coroner Downsen leads Carin into a storage room that he has turned into a workroom. The white lab coat hides the coroner's fitness. A bright face under a mop of dark hair is easy on the eyes. Carin eyes the wedding band and stops evaluating Marc.

Thirteen file folders are organized on the table centered in a valley of shelves piled high with boxes. Each folder is open to a summary on the left and an image of the deceased on the right. Carin likes Downsen. Carin likes meticulousness. Carin reconfirms the wedding band.

Shoving aside the creepy feeling of being surrounded by dozens of boxes labeled with hundreds of names and dates of death, Carin examines the folders Downsen has arranged for display.

"The files date back just under two years. Tell me what you see."

"They have all been shot in the heart."

"Shot or pierced. What else?"

"Are they all women? That can't be right."

"No, three are men. Keep looking."

Marc struggles to wait patiently for Carin to scan each summary and image for a clue he hopes she'll find.

"These notes you added are interesting. You think the first eight died when someone pierced the heart with an unknown device. These five are different. Those parallel marks on the chest? They all have the same marks. What are they?"

"Good eye. We weren't sure. All deaths before Marjory Mosen are classified as natural causes or attributed to an illness. Cancer got most of them. I've been here a year. The coroner before me wrote off the chest wounds as revival attempts with a paddle or a needle."

"The coroner before you was McKinnon. Right?"

"Yes."

"Any relation to Jared McKinnon of the McKinnon Funeral Home?"

"The senior McKinnon died right in this storeroom — from a heart attack with no one around. I think my predecessor was Jared McKinnon Senior. Why?"

"Nothing. Maybe. Something I learned a couple of days ago. The marks?"

"I sent the images and summaries to several colleagues who looked at them, and no one is sure what could have made those impressions in the skin."

"You didn't get me down here to guess. Thirteen people with odd marks is not a coincidence. What's your theory?"

"The killer used the ICS to reach the heart."

Carin looks at the images and asks.

"ICS?"

"The Intercostal Space is the soft area between ribs. The parallel marks and the entry wounds are over an ICS. Also, either they were dead when shot, or they died from the bullet. An off-the-shelf .22 would probably exit the body. These people were shot with a round modified to enter the heart and stop short of exiting the body."

"Come on, Marc. That can't be possible."

"Everything is possible if you try hard enough. Someone used a bullet with enough kinetic energy to stop a heart and not leave an exit wound. After the bullet destroyed the heart, the killer pressed a device to the chest."

"Marc, this had better not be a heart-eating ritual."

"No, nothing like that. I think the killer created a device to extract the bullet. Those parallel indents in the skin are the feet of the device. Place the device over the entrance wound, lower a grapple, and fish out the bullet. Also, no powder burns were noted in the files. Someone cleaned the wounds. Assuming they are bullet wounds."

Scanning the images again and considering Marc's words, Carin is impressed.

"Look closely at that one."

Carin follows where Marc is pointing, then leans toward the image.

"What should I see?"

"The skin. Plastiskin or double-sided tape made that right angle mark. Someone put a patch over the heart before killing the patient."

"Why?"

"To collect powder residue and shell fragments."

"I think you're correct. Someone has a strong understanding of firearm ballistics. Marc, do you know what this means?"

"Senior McKinnon either missed the connections, ignored the data, or hid information about the deaths. Either way, we know now. There is an active serial killer, and he is taking trophies."

"Where do you send the unclaimed bodies?"

"After we secure samples, we send them to a mortuary for cremation and storage."

"Samples?"

"Blood, skin, brain, hair, dental x-rays, anything that may be needed later if the death was not from natural causes."

"Yuk. Creepy."

"To you. For me, it's another day at the office."

Carin spins to leave the morgue yet turns a full circle to ask.

"One more thing."

"What, are you Columbo now?"

"Har. Har. Which mortuary gets the unclaimed bodies?"

"It is a rotating list of eight, maybe ten facilities in our area. We are the coroner's office for Hemingway, Twekonda, and Juinera counties. When a facility name reaches the top of the list, they are the next call. They go to the bottom of the list if they can process the body. They stay at the top of the list if they can't take the body."

"Spreading the county money around. Good system. What do you want to bet Old Man McKinnon didn't rotate the list?"

"No bet."

"What about a bet on Old Man McKinnon ignoring the marks on the chest? Who wants the police poking around your under-the-counter cash cow?"

"No bet. It looks like the McKinnons had a good thing going."

"Without Daddy's help, Jared McKinnon is probably desperate to keep his businesses financially viable. Keep the bullet retrieval theory to yourself. If true, Jared McKinnon being in financial trouble is high on the list of motives. Please keep a lid on the information. You and me only. No one else hears about this until I speak to the chief and hold a press conference. Marc, I am serious. We are buttoned up tight on this until we have a solid lead. If this leaks, we'll be in hot water, and the press will be up our asses. Serial killers are FBI business. Keep it quiet until I talk to the chief."

"Wow, I guess you want me to keep this quiet. Understood. Carin, what about the folks down the hall? The forensics team knows a lot about the bodies."

"What are you asking?"

"You know what I'm asking."

The images of thirteen bodies flip like a family album in Carin's mind. At the same time, she contemplates her response to the coroner.

"Our people are good and work hard. This is above their skill set. The forensics team lead isn't interested in learning new techniques. Retirement is on his radar, not advanced forensic methodologies. Marc, the FBI will be here soon, and their forensics people will help."

"Our people will not like the Feds taking over and reviewing their work."

"No, they won't like an outside review. We have no choice. When the chief makes the call, and he will, we'll be kicked to the curb. Also, just so we're clear and working with full disclosure, I am a proponent of physician-assisted suicide. I think the Scandinavian countries have a good system. I am not a supporter of murder, no matter how well-intentioned it might appear. Killing people like this is murder."

"Agreed. It would help if you found whoever is doing the killing. Before the Feds show up and kick you to the curb."

"Tell me something I don't know."

Chapter Six

Standing at a podium with the Hemingway County seal on the front, Carin is providing a run-down of the investigation.

The new detective had a vision and a hope that her first press conference would be a room full of eager reporters, all vying for her attention. Three people, one of whom appears to be a busybody and not a reporter, are a disappointing number of attendees. An unattended camera is recording the session. She chalks it up to another lesson in the life of a detective in a rural community.

"That is all I have for you at this time. In summary, we are investigating several recent deaths. We will ensure you have the information we can share when we learn more. You are first."

"What about the chest wounds?"

"Who are you?"

"I am Irene Sunderland from the *Marble Grove Gazette*."

"Irene, there are wounds on the bodies that are consistent with recovery efforts by the first responders."

"Were the victims shot?"

"We have not yet confirmed the cause of death. Yes, you?"

"Norv Wenderling, *Hemingway Reports*. Detective Trimble, have you discovered anything unusual about the recent deaths?"

"Norv, I am not familiar with *Hemingway Reports*."

"Hemingway Reports *dot com*. It is an online

newspaper. That is my camera. We are being streamed live."

Carin's eyes follow Norv's finger, pointing to the unattended camera on a tripod.

"I see. You are asking if we have discovered anything unusual about the recent deaths. Can you be more specific?"

"Detective, were the deaths connected in any way?"

"At this time, we are researching all possible leads. That's it for today. When I know more, you will know more."

Before Carin leaves the podium, Irene Sunderland grumbles.

"Your predecessor doesn't think you can do the job."

With a smile, Carin bites back.

"People have been underestimating me my whole life. This job is no different — I will prove them wrong."

Irene clicks off her recorder, smiles, and winks at Detective Trimble, ending the press conference.

Al is watching the afternoon news in his apartment from the desk chair. He focuses on the person filling the screen — the chyron reads Detective Carin Trimble. Upset that Carin didn't reference a serial killer or mention his name, Al decides to email the detective with additional details about the diverse murders.

It takes Al three hours to create the email and send it.

Three hours — not because Al wants to withhold information from Carin. It takes so long because Al wants credit for solving the serial killer murders. He worked hard on the email to ask for credit without directly accusing the detective of stealing his information.

Detective Carin,

You did not mention the team that is assisting you in the investigation. Is there a reason you are not talking about your team to the news people?

Al

Unfortunately, two days passed with no response from the detective. Al's parents struggle to keep their son calm and focused at dinner. Of course, Mrs. Demchuk's dinner routine is part of a lifestyle that is rapidly fading from American culture. His wife's insistence on hosting dinner, at the formal table every night at six, grates on John Demchuk. Their son Al accepts the routine as the usual daily process.

"Dad, call Uncle Myron."

"Al, stop smashing the peas with your knife. I am sure Detective Trimble is not ignoring you. She is busy with the case and probably other cases."

Al's knife pushes mashed peas onto the linen tablecloth. Looking at his mother, hoping she does not have one of her moments, then picking up the smashed peas, Al puts his hands flat on the table. Dad speaks before Deena can gripe.

"Al, give it a couple of days."

"Dad, I could call Uncle Myron."

"No, Al. You know very well your uncle prefers to be called Al. What did your Uncle *Al* tell you? What did I tell you about using people's correct names? Remember when you knew who painted the penis on the water tower? You had names, not proof. What did Al say?"

"He said to let the professionals do their job."

No murders for a few weeks and the clues running dry have put Carin in a foul mood. The detective decides there is more to Al's information.

"How was Al able to connect the deaths for his reports? Where is he getting his information? I need to know more about ASD. How do I interact better with a self-appointed assistant?"

Deciding to visit a center known for developing employment and living options for adults with autism is the first step in learning more about Al.

According to the bronze plaque on the wall in the foyer, the Pritchett Center for Autism and Neurodiversity Support has been in operation for twenty-five years. Reading the message emblazoned on the opposite wall in the lobby, Carin realizes she agrees with the center's motto: *An independent life is a future everyone deserves.*

After meeting with several doctors and people with varying levels of ASD and collecting a pile of educational brochures, Carin has a new appreciation for the people on the spectrum. The Doctors are full of hope and optimism. The patients she met were gracious and seemed to like questioning the detective about being an investigator. Also, Carin learned the center was located in Marble Grove using a county tax incentive program. The quarry closing and the bus line dropping Marble Grove from its route badly hurt the local economy. The county and the town did whatever they could to keep the commerce flowing.

About to open the door and exit the center, Carin is stunned and a little afraid to see the silhouette of a stocky man cross the window. Stepping onto the sidewalk, she finds the man waiting for her.

Carin sees Al's agitation. Something about how he is trying to act normal convinces her to listen. The person who put her onto the serial killer thread is forcibly making eye contact and trying to look nonchalant. Accepting reality, the detective is learning quickly. Her new *assistant* is a shockingly good hacker.

"Detective Carin." Interrupting, Carin is firm yet kind.

"Al, I want you to tell me how you knew I was at the center."

"Laura told me."

"Laura? Who is Laura?"

"She is in there."

Knowing the ASD facility is behind her, Carin reacts to Al's pointing and is annoyed with herself when she turns and looks at what she knows is behind her. Huffing, her focus goes back on Al, and she uses the skills she learned in training to control her voice. The detective continues questioning Al.

"Laura is in the center? I don't remember meeting a Laura. Help me understand."

"Laura is my friend."

"Laura is your friend. Why did your friend tell you I was visiting the center?"

"Laura knows I am helping you."

Carin turns again when Al waves to the building. A woman Carin can't quite see is waving back at Al from a window.

"Al, is that Laura?"

"Yes."

"She called you?"

"No."

"No? Then how did Laura contact you?"

"She uses emails and sends the texts."

"I see."

"Laura doesn't talk."

"Ah, that is good information. Al, it is inappropriate for you to follow me. Why are you here?"

"I saw you."

"Where did you see me?"

"On the news."

"The press conference? That was two weeks ago."

"Nine days. Press conference."

"What about the press conference?"

"You lied."

"I didn't lie. What are you talking about?"

"You didn't say there is a serial killer. A doctor is killing people with terminated cancer. You didn't tell people. You lied."

"The word is *terminal*. I think you know that. Al, Let's go into that café."

Carin points across the street to a boutique little restaurant whose painted window claims to be the winner of the best scones at the Minnesota State Fair — three years running. A half dozen tables inside, another four on the sidewalk, are filled. The bakery smells pleasing and welcoming as she and Al arrive at the café's door.

"Look, those people are leaving. We can sit outside and discuss why I didn't tell people everything at the press conference."

After convincing Al to order tea, Carin is happy with the sidewalk table beside the window and away from other people. Setting her phone on the wire mesh table, Carin begins as Al tucks his backpack under the table, between his feet.

"I'm your friend. You know that, right?"

"Yes."

"Maybe you and I can go to the center together — sometime. It's a place where people learn the skills needed to live well. You are doing well. Maybe the center has some new ideas. We all need people to help us now and then. I have my work team, workout partners, and friends from the Marines and college. Al, having a support team is always good. Do you want to make a new team and learn new things?"

"Learn? I've been to that center. Laura is my friend. I don't need a doctor. I don't want another doctor."

"No, not a doctor. It's a center that helps people with their abilities. There are people there who are like you. Men and women. You know all this. Why don't you want to go to the center?"

"Are you fixing me up?"

"No! If you don't want to go to the center, okay. It was just an idea. First, I want you to agree to something."

"Look."

Al points to a small bird that landed on the back of an empty chair. The bird arrived when the waitress set down coffee for Carin, tea for Al, and a complimentary scone cut in half to share. Carin deduces the server must be a summer temporary worker.

"Thank you for the scone. What is it?"

"Melba is trying a new flavor. It's lemon-raspberry."

With a smile, the server departs. The bird remains — intent on examining Al, Carin, and the scones.

"Yes, Al, finches and sparrows learn people drop crumbs on the tables and sidewalk. I want you to agree."

"Agree to what?"

"If you want to be my assistant, tell me how you learned about the murders."

"Partner."

"I don't understand?"

"I want to be your partner like in the TV shows. There

are always two detectives. Partner."

"Okay, Al, you will be my unofficial partner. You can be my partner only if you tell me how you learned about the murders."

Looking across, less than half a block down the street, Carin is sure Laura is watching Al from a window. Al follows Carin's eyes, turns, quickly waves to Laura, and then turns back and nervously looks everywhere that is not Carin.

"Al, is Laura your girlfriend?"

"No."

"Do you want her to be your girlfriend?"

"People like me don't have girlfriends."

"You are wrong. I think Laura wants to be your girlfriend. You mentioned that you exchanged texts with Laura."

"Yes."

"What do you talk about in the texts?"

"The cases."

"You exchange texts with Laura about the murders?"

"Yes."

"I understand. I think. Does Laura help you find the victims?"

"No."

"You haven't tried your scone."

Al picks off a small piece of the triangular pastry's corner, puts it in his mouth, and then smiles.

"It's good, right?"

"It is okay. Partner."

"You can be my *unofficial* partner only if you tell me how you found the information about the victims. Do you think there will be another victim soon? Should we warn someone or someplace to be more careful with their security?"

Al is pinching off tiny bits of scone to eat and waiting for people to pass before answering.

"Yes."

"Are you sure? Al, are you *very* sure?"

"Yes."

Carin waits for Al to eat a couple more pieces of his half of the scone. Also, she notes that Laura is still watching from the window.

"Laura is interested in Al." Keeping her thoughts to herself, Carin adopts a friendlier tone.

"Okay, partner. Do you know what partners have?"

"No."

"Partners have trust. Do you trust me?"

"I trust you."

"If you trust me, and I certainly trust you, then we must share information. It is part of the partner code."

"Code?"

"Unwritten rules of being partners. Do you know what unwritten rules are?"

"Things that are true. Things not written on paper."

"Exactly right. If you want to be my partner, you must follow the unwritten rules. Rule one: Partners share everything."

Carin waits, letting Al think and munch on another

piece of the stiff pastry. Eventually, he swallows, looks up quickly, catches Carin looking back, then looks back down.

"I have the passwords."

"Passwords to what?"

"HIPPY."

"You have the passwords to an information system under the HIPAA regulations?"

"Yes."

Carin suppresses the panic that rises in her mind.

"Al, listen to me. Look at me. Please. Okay. Never tell anyone else that you have the passwords. Never. You must understand what I am telling you. Do you understand?"

"It is against the laws for me to have the passwords."

"That is correct. You already know that it is probably illegal for you to have the passwords. Never tell me how you got them. Do you understand?"

"It is my secret."

"Yes, it is your secret. If we are going to be partners, I need to know I can trust you. Al, can I trust you?"

"Yes. Can I trust you? Detective Carin."

Taken aback at the implication being turned on her, Carin's respect for her unofficial partner deepens. There is a lot more intelligence within Al than she expected. He wants the world to see him as a bright man with ambition and a capable detective.

"I learned something in the ASD facility. Many people with ASD, like you, are brilliant. Sometimes, their thinking becomes confused. That's why some of the words you use are not correct. I know your secret. Sometimes, you deliberately use the wrong words. If we're partners, you have to use the correct words. No playing games."

"Partners."

"I'll take that as agreement. Do you have any information on who might be the next victim?"

Reaching down without looking, pulling the zipper, and reaching inside, Al pulls a folder from his backpack and slides across a single-page report. Careful to miss the drop of spilled tea, Al ensured the page was clean and dry when it reached Carin.

Chapter Seven

Case ID :	A-114
Name of Deceased :	Tercia Marie LeClare
Date of Report :	19-Jul-23
Cause of Death :	
Place of Death :	
Date of Death :	
Time of Death :	
Investigator :	Marcus Alvin Demchuk

Background

Details

1)
2)
3)

The report is incomplete and problematic to the detective.

"Has Al taken the criticism about his reporting too far?"

Carin gently guides her unofficial partner in reviewing the sparse information.

"Tercia Marie LeClare. What makes you think she's the next victim on the murderer's list?"

"Terminated cancer."

"Al, *Partner*, use the right words. What kind of *terminal* cancer?"

"Lung cancer. Baby cancer."

"Do you mean ovarian cancer?"

"Yes."

"Let's step back a little. I looked at your other reports and the updates you emailed to me. The correlation between your reports is accurate. However, nothing is concrete."

Pausing, letting a couple pass, then shooing away the sparrow eying her uneaten half of the drying pastry, Carin continues in a low voice meant only for Al.

"Officially, most people in your reports died from illnesses or natural causes. Al, nothing in your reports names a suspect or suspects. You have not provided a list of names of people you think are of interest. Do you have a list of names you think might be people we should look at for the murders? Also, *Partner*, can you speak up? The breeze makes it hard for me to hear your soft voice."

"Correlation."

Keeping her voice soft and calm is a way for Carin to control her frustration.

"I don't understand."

"You used the word correlation. Correlation?"

"Oh. Sorry. Correlation means connected. None of the victims in your reports are connected."

"Connected?" The detective gives Al a moment to process the new word.

"Yes, connected. Did any of the victims in your reports know each other?"

"No."

"Then finding the killer is going to be more difficult. If we had anything linking the victims, any correlation, we would have a lead to follow."

Carin pauses while Al tries to convince a sparrow eyeing his scone to lite on his finger. Unsuccessful, he reluctantly shoos the bird from his lemon-raspberry goodness. Grinning to herself, the detective continues.

"If we can identify facilities that seem like good candidates for the killer to strike next, we can alert the staff to be watchful and perhaps set up some surveillance equipment. We'll start with Tercia Marie LeClare. Where is Tercia?"

"Don't know."

"That's okay. I'll find out. We might not be able to prevent another person from dying. We'll try like hell to guess at the next location and have a better chance of catching the killer."

Carin makes a call while watching Al eat tiny bits of scone.

"Yes, this is Detective Trimble, authorization code: Alpha-Five-November-X-Ray. Thank you. I need the location history for Tercia Marie LeClare, DOB unknown. There is not likely to be more than one Tercia Marie LeClare anywhere near Hemingway County. Good, thank you. Send me a text."

Putting away her phone and, following years of military bearing, ensuring her shirt is tucked in tight, Carin rises to leave.

"Alpha-Five-November-X-Ray. DOB unknown. You like white shirts."

"Huh?"

"Detective Carin. You always wear white shirts with the lines in the front."

"Lines? You mean the stitched creases. I like white shirts. Partner, go home. Find out who is going to be next. We can stop the killer."

Al leaves a large piece of his scone and tea when he silently walks away. Carin catches her new partner's slight wave to Laura in the window halfway down the block.

* * *
** ** **

Visiting long-term healthcare facilities, retirement homes, hospices, and the morgue is wearing on Carin's psyche. Using her training from the counseling sessions to push aside the thoughts of her mortality, she arrives to interview the person Al reported to be next on the killer's list.

"At least the paint is not flaking from the walls, and the windows have been cleaned. This facility is a step up."

A man, slightly taller than her, probably five-foot-eight, about the same build, wearing khakis and a blue polo shirt, removes his hand from the shoulder of a youngish female receptionist and steps from behind the counter.

"Hello, I'm Detective Trimble. Mr. Jensen, thank you for agreeing to meet me. How long have you been the manager here at Guardian Heart Hospice?"

"About three months."

"As I mentioned on the phone, I'm gathering background for my investigation. I'd like to talk to one of your patients."

"Guests. We don't have patients. We have guests."

"One of your *guests* is Tercia Marie LeClare."

"I remember — you mentioned the name on the phone. Miss LeClare is in room one-eighteen."

"I presume one-eighteen is down that hall?"

"Yes, down the hall, turn left, then the second right. It is the last room on the left. I'll show you."

"No need. I want to visit Miss LeClare alone. If, that is okay?"

"Sure. I'll wait here. Technically, we close to visitors in a few minutes. We open again for visitation after the dinner hour, from seven to ten. I will wait for you to complete your visit."

* * *
** ** **

Rounding the corner, Carin notices every other light is dark. *"Are all long-term care facilities struggling financially?"*

Pushing into room one-eighteen, a scuffle catches Carin's ear. A dark flash piercing the corner of her eye is what she remembers after waking up to Al's voice.

"Detective Carin, you are awake."

"Al? What happened?"

Carin realizes she is in room one-eighteen as she lifts herself from the floor. The detective is trying to work out if she is just dazed or unconscious. She does not remember talking to Tercia LeClare — who Carin sees is in her bed, dead, presumably from cancer, not shot. Woozy, rubbing the back and side of her head, Carin looks around and lands on Al, who is uncharacteristically looking back from the doorway.

"Someone knocked you in the head. I told you she would shoot you. She knocked you in the head. See, I told you."

"You never told me someone would shoot me. Please, calm down. How long have you been here? How did you get in?"

"When you are like me, if you throw the right kind of tantrum, people will give you what you want or leave you alone. Mr. Jensen, let me in because I am your partner."

Rubbing her head, further considering the idea that Al uses his disability as a tool, Carin steps closer to the body of Miss LeClare. Adding to her growing suspicions about Al, the idea that her new partner might have hit her on the head is unsettling.

Eyeing the body and rubbing her head, Carin gently begins her questions.

"How long have you been here?"

"Not long."

"Did you see anyone else in the room? Did you see

anyone in the hallway? Did you pass anyone coming down the hall?"

"No. Do you believe me now? We have to go."

"You said *she*. Before, you said it was a male doctor killing people. Do you have new information?"

"No. Do you believe me now? We have to go."

"*Partner*, we need to keep the attack confidential. Please do not talk about someone hitting me in the head. Do you understand?"

"Confidential information is a secret."

"Okay. Good. I think. I checked the police file for the reports you gave me. None of the murders were committed during the day. They were all in the overnight hours. I think the murderer was here. This time, however, it doesn't look like the killer murdered Miss LeClare."

Pausing, considering, Carin reminds herself that a good detective is not shy and will ask hard questions. Standing tall, facing her shorter partner, the detective asks.

"Al, did you hit me in the head?"

"No."

Not expecting a simple response, something she learned at the ASD facility flashes into Carin's mind. People with ASD are often literal and do not respond negatively to social clues that might offend others. She begins thinking out loud for Al's benefit.

"Something has changed. The murderer changed tactics or was running a recon mission."

"Recon?"

"The murderer was reviewing the facility to create a

plan to kill Tercia. Al, it's our secret. Okay?"

"Secret. Do you believe me now? We have to go."

Ignoring Al's increasing agitation. His swaying and movement remind her of the people she met at the Pritchett Center. Deciding to use her calmness to help Al cope, Carin stops speaking. She notices the room is sparse. There are no family pictures to indicate that Tercia LeClare was loved. Leaning over the bed and using a folded vinyl glove pulled from her pocket, Carin presses the call button. Mr. Jensen and a nurse-caretaker enter the room in less than a minute. Carin meekly nods toward the bed and the body.

"It appears Miss LeClare has passed."

Pacing, wringing his hands, sweating, bobbing, Al is on edge. Carin demanding that he keep secrets was tough enough for the man. His partner stating Miss LeClare was dead, tipped Al into a mild panic.

"Relax, Al. Death is natural. Mr. Jensen, I will take my friend into the lobby."

"Partner."

"Yes, Al, partner. Mr. Jensen, I'll wait for you to remove the body. This room is at the end of the hall, next to the emergency exit. Do you know if the alarm on the crash bar works?"

"I have no clue. Let's see."

Carin, Al, and Jensen exit Tercia's room and enter the hallway, leaving the nurse-caretaker to manage the body. Jensen pushes the crash bar, causing the door to swing open and exposing a strip of asphalt wide enough for delivery trucks. The forest beyond the asphalt is green and lush.

Dozens of cigarette butts pushed against the bricks by the wind are a clue. The residents use this area to smoke. Carin's suspicion is quickly confirmed. The door opens from the outside. No alarm from pressing the crash bar and a security door that opens from the outside is cause for Carin to raise an eyebrow toward Jensen. Al interrupts before Carin can speak.

"Detective Carin, we need to go."

"Al, hold on a second. Thank you, Mr. Jensen. I am sure you will have the security measures brought up to code. Do you have a business card?"

He takes a card out of his pocket and hands it to her.

Al holds out his hand, expecting a business card. Jenson looks to Carin, who nods towards Al — Jensen gives Al a card. Carin twists a wry facial thank-you before closing the discussion.

"Thanks. If I need anything, I'll call or email."

"Detective Carin, we need to go."

"Go? Al, slow down. Look at me. Go where?"

Behind Jensen's back, Carin puts her finger to her lips. Carin pulls Al through the emergency door, allowing it to close, and begins walking around the building. She scans the area for security cameras and clues while heading in the general direction of their cars. Her quiet approach forces Al to follow.

"Do you believe me now? Detective Carin, she tried to kill you."

"I believe you. He or she, which is it? You know you don't have to call me *Detective Carin*. We're partners. You can call me Carin. Al, you said *she.* Do you know where the next murder will occur? Do you know who's killing these people?"

"Maybe. Yes. Maybe. Detective Carin, we have to go. I have to update my report. We have to go."

Watching Al writhe and fret, compounding her painful headache, Carin realizes the blow to her head may have cost her short-term memory. Also, Al is panicked by the LeClare death, being close to a dead body and a murderer.

"Slow down. Partner, I need to understand why you're worried. What are you not saying?"

Before Al can respond, as the duo rounds the corner to the front of the building, Mr. Jensen emerges from the main entrance. Al steps toward the trees, veering away from the conversation.

"Detective, I checked, and I thought you should know. Miss LeClare will be taken to the McKinnon mortuary for care. She is scheduled for cremation. Unless you need something else?"

"Why are there no security cameras on the backside of the building?"

"Money. Is there ever any other reason? Do you need anything else?"

"No, nothing else. Thank you. Wait! Yes. I will have the body examined. I know she probably died from cancer. I would not be a detective if I didn't check all possibilities. I'll have the body moved to the coroner's office. Also, those security cameras, where is the video stored?"

"In the control room. We have the parking lot, the

entrance, the lobby, and the hallways on security."

"I'll have my team copy the video if that's okay. If not, I'll get a warrant."

"They need to get here quickly. The video is on a twenty-four-hour overwrite cycle."

Carin makes the call to the forensics team and then turns to Al, waiting for Mr. Jensen to be far enough away.

"Something is up with him. This is the worst he has been with the ticks and movements."

"Partner, let's talk. I need you to relax. We have a case to discuss. I'll find a new partner if you don't want to help."

Al silently walks toward his car, with Carin following.

"I know you used the word *she*. What did you mean?"

"The doctor killing terminated patients is a girl."

"The murderer is probably not a girl. A *woman* is more likely to be the person of interest. Assuming you're correct, where did you find the name?"

"No name."

"You don't have a name. Al, do you think the killer is a woman?"

"A woman."

"Why do you think the killer is a woman?"

"Nurse."

"I don't understand. Help me understand."

"The killer dresses up like a nurse."

Carin immediately connects the dots.

"Did you see someone in the hallway or Miss LeClare's room?"

"No."

Carin makes the mental leap that she knows is problematic if true.

"Partner, you have heard me ask about security footage at the murder locations. Did you do something?"

Al leans and sways, staring at the trees and not answering. His movements remind Carin of the people she visited in the facility. The silence is the detective's confirmation.

"Do you have security camera footage from here or other facilities? Did you find video images of the killer?"

"Partner."

"Of course. Partner, did you get access to security camera footage of the killer?"

"Yes."

"The person in the images is a woman?"

"A nurse."

"How do you know it is a female nurse?"

"I know."

"Partner, you cannot let people know you've hacked a security system. It is not legal, and no court would accept the images as evidence. We can use the information to find another way to prove who the killer is and how to stop the next murder."

"I didn't steal the movies."

"What do you mean you didn't steal the security footage? Please explain it to me."

Al listens to several birds, forcing Carin to wait. Patience is the best option when communicating with Al.

"Detective Carin."

"That's me. Partner, is there something you want to tell me?"

"McKinnon Funeral Home and Mortuary."

"What about it?"

"Password."

"Al, are you saying their computer systems are not password protected?"

"Password is password."

"Will you email the video to me?"

"Too big."

"The video files are too big to email?"

Al pulls a flash drive from his backpack and hands it to Carin.

"Thank you. I will look at it later. Al, can I ask you something?"

"Yes."

"Do you always wear T-shirts with comic book characters on the front?"

"Yes."

"That's nice. You wore a collared shirt the first time we met. Now you are back to the T-shirts."

"We are partners."

"That is true, and partners are comfortable with each other."

Mari and Ash pull to a stop in their response vehicle. An ambulance on steroids, Carin is sure Mari likes driving the beast of a truck. Mari rolls down the driver's window, leans out, and gives Al and Carin a massive grin.

"We have to stop meeting like this. People are going to

start talking."

"Let them talk. Take the body to the morgue. Tell Marc Downsen I need this exam to be next."

Mari beams, her eyes twinkling, then sits forward and drives off to find a spot large enough to park the beast. Carin wonders if Mari was giving her an opening to chat.

"Al?"

"Partner."

"Partner, do you know who will be next?"

"Maybe."

Chapter Eight

"Kel, are you home?"

"Yes."

Prepping for another workday, Louie is hollering from the bedroom when she hears the door close with Kel and Booger returning from their morning walk. Feeling guilty about being away from home for work, Kel walks his love's dog most mornings and every evening when he's home. In the bedroom, stripping quickly to his birthday suit, Kel doesn't step into the shower. Instead, he puts on a show for Louie.

"Yes, Kel, I see it."

Exasperated, Louie grins anyway and pushes her man toward the shower, stepping closer to the dresser and her earrings.

"Stop flopping it at me. Go shower. I don't have time. I don't want to be late for work. You know Mondays are the worst."

"Come on. We'll be quick."

"No. I have two new patients this morning, and you know how that goes. Kel, you were up all night. How did the release go? Did the application crash and burn?"

"No, smarty farty, it didn't crash and burn. There were a few issues. Nothing serious."

Turning to her man, securing an earring, and ignoring the nakedness, Louie's tone is serious.

"No more trips?"

"That's not what I said. There will be fewer trips now

that the application is in production. I don't have to hover over the cubicles to keep people focused. Lou, come on, we'll be quick."

"I don't have time. Get in the shower. First, promise you will be home for a few weeks."

"I promise."

"Kel?"

"Lou, I have a two-day trip planned for the week after next. Then a two-day trip at the end of next month. That's it for now. I told you I would cut the trips from three days to two, and I did. My promise is to limit being away as much as possible. Now, doesn't this look like fun?"

"Seeing you nekkid is not always fun. How about we make it a date night? If you play your cards correctly, you might get lucky. I have to go to work."

* * *

Happy she's not in another nursing home, Carin has scheduled an interview with Dr. Greene and PA Mancone. Greene heads an oncology clinic at the regional hospital, and understanding cancer is Carin's new focus for the murder investigation.

"Why do so many murder victims have ties to Dr. Greene?"

"Hello, I'm Detective Trimble. I believe we spoke on the phone."

"Dr. Greene and PA Mancone are with patients. They will be available in a few minutes. Dr. Greene requested I ask you to wait in the conference room. Can I get you anything to drink?"

"No, thank you."

It is forty minutes of scrolling mindlessly on her phone before Dr. Greene and PA Mancone arrive and take seats across the table from Carin. Despite the white medical coats with their names embroidered in blue on the left breast, neither is what Carin expected. Greene is average in every possible way except her hair. With no makeup or nail polish and sporting a neon pink crewcut, Doctor of Oncology Sharon Greene is making a statement. In contrast, the tall PA Lauren Mancone's jet-black hair is in a ponytail. Her hair ends just above her waist, held tight with scrunchies and trimmed so she doesn't sit on it.

"Hello, I'm Detective Trimble. Thank you for taking the time to speak with me."

"What is this about?"

"Dr. Greene, in the research for a case I am working on, your names appeared several times. Can you answer a few background questions for me?"

"Case?"

"Yes, an investigation. Dr. Greene, is your clinic part of Hemingway County Medical Center?"

"Yes. I receive office, lab, and clinic space from the Medical Center. What is this about?"

"I believe you can provide some information about prior patients. First, your clinic receives space from the Medical Center. According to the website, your funding comes from big-pharmaceutical company grants."

"So what? Big Pharma funds thousands of studies. Did

you clear this with Legal? I am sure the Medical Center does not want the bad publicity that comes with a murder investigation."

"Um, no. I don't think a simple conversation requires attorney approval."

"A detective should know that HIPAA prevents discussion of patients with anyone who is not on the release forms. You should talk to Legal and then schedule a chat. The law is clear. Are we done?"

"I am aware of the HIPAA regulations. I am not asking you to violate confidentiality. Just a few questions."

"We'll see."

Suddenly, the spacious conference room feels tight and narrow to the detective. Carin eyes the wary doctor before she pulls up her notes using her phone.

"Can you confirm Marjory Ellen Mosen, Mary-Ethel Smyth, Candice Alice Bretherton, and Tercia Marie LeClare were your patients? All have recently passed, and we are trying to establish their activities in the days and weeks before they passed."

"Who my patients are, or are not, is not something I can discuss. They didn't pass. Those women were murdered. We are done here."

Carin catches Mancone squirming at Greene's nasty response. She chooses to say nothing and alters her approach with Greene.

"I am sorry for the misstatement, Dr. Greene. Tercia LeClare passed. We are still trying to determine the cause of death for the others."

"You know what killed the women. The victims were shot in the heart. Same as the others."

"I see you are aware of the murders."

"I called Marc Downsen."

"Oh?"

Sharon Greene, MD, sits silently, without any hint of compassion or concern. Carin presses the doctor.

"Please expand on your conversation with the coroner."

Greene sits silently under her pink hair. Carin realizes she is losing patience with the doctor. The former Marine remembers the counseling she received to control her temper. She keeps her voice neutral.

"Dr. Greene, I have probable cause for a warrant to compel you to speak with me. I'll come back with a deputy and do this the hard way. If that's what you prefer."

Mancone's squirming says everything. Greene begins another tart response.

"When I saw your press conference, I knew some victims were in my pain trial. Knowing the victims murdered alters the results of the trial. Confirming their identity with the coroner was confirmation for adjusting the data for my pain trial. I am telling you that because you can learn from their families that they were patients in my trial. That is all you are going to get without a warrant."

"I feel you might have additional information that could be useful in my investigation. Any information you can share could be helpful."

"I suggest you speak to Legal. My take is Legal will tell you to get a subpoena. Are we done?"

"One more question. Why does it seem to me that you are unconcerned about your patients? Using your term, unconcerned about your patients being *murdered*? It seems to me that a caregiver would have empathy for the victims."

"Detective Trimble, I don't have time to express empathy or consideration to you or anyone else whose business it is to pry into the personal grief of others. What I think or feel is none of your concern."

"I'm sorry to have bothered you. Thank you for your time, Dr. Greene. Mrs. Mancone."

Before Carin can rise from her seat, Greene continues speaking in a biting tone.

"Whoever shot those people did them and their families a favor. Do you know how bad it is for people living with cancer when our powerful pain drugs stop working? Do you have any idea about the agony these people endure? No, of course, you don't. You are like most people. You don't understand. Those *people* weren't murdered — they were released. Those *people* were living with the evil that was destroying their bodies. Those *people* were released from unimaginable pain. Those *people* have families that are now free from the daily torment of the suffering endured by loved ones. Detective Trimble, murder is not the answer. Sometimes, now and again, releasing someone from their torture is the right choice. I have patients to see. Goodbye, Detective Trimble."

Carin catches PA Mancone's eye behind Dr. Greene's back. Louie looks like she wants to stop and speak. Instead, she shakes her head in the negative and follows her boss through the door.

* * *

Called into the chief's office, confident she is about to receive a slap on the wrist, Carin slumps into the chair.

Chief Myron Albert Johnston is the first police chief in Hemingway County's 176 years who is not related to a considerable percentage of the local population. Not stereotypical for a rural community, Chief Johnston is a person of color and speaks with technical confidence. He readily accepts new technologies and policing techniques. Johnston is a one-person crusade to revamp the MGHPD. The chief rolling his finger in the air with a short question is Carin's cue to begin her summary.

"What have you got?"

"So far, fourteen dead. Thirteen murdered. Shot or stabbed in the heart. No witnesses. No ballistics. No suspects. Someone is playing Dr. Kevorkian."

"Being shot in the heart is not the same as drug-induced euthanasia."

"No, Chief, I suppose it isn't. You have my reports. What's up?"

"You can't go around pestering doctors for information. The hospital's lawyers called me. The lawyers must be in the room if you want to talk to their employees. No exceptions."

"I got it. Just so you know, Chief, I didn't ask Greene or

Mancone to violate confidentiality. Greene didn't like me finding out the victims had been through her clinic."

"That's not an odd connection. The victims were cancer patients — making a correlation with the clinic is a reasonable conclusion. Do you think Greene is a person of interest?"

"Not yet. Maybe. I need to find the common link. I have to pull on the thread that is Greene and Mancone."

"Understood. Carin?"

"Yes, Chief?"

"Three days. I called the Feds. They will be here in three days. Find something, or the case will be taken away."

Carin realizes her boss is giving her time to solve the case. It is a gift with an expiration date.

"A week. I got it, Chief."

"*Three days* or we'll have the Feds up our ass. Also, who is Al?"

"Al? Why do you ask?"

"Because I received an email from Marcus Alvin Demchuk. This person, Al, says he is your *partner*."

"He is my partner in name only. Al is an amateur detective and has information about the victims. Because Al is on the autism spectrum, I humor his desire to 'assist' me. And, it is always good to be nice."

Carin's air quotes at the word assist were unnecessary. She felt the chief needed to know she was keeping Al at arm's length.

"This Al person is assisting you? How?"

"He creates these reports about deaths he finds on the

internet. It was Al who thought maybe the people with cancer were linked. He was correct. Don't worry, Chief. I don't tell him anything that would create a legal problem. I'm confused. Why did Al send an email to you? Did he complain about me? What was the complaint?"

The chief quickly types a few things, nods to what he found on the PC, looks up with a wry grin, and lets Carin in on the secret.

"He says you're not taking him seriously enough. Let me read you what he wrote: *'Detective Carin is not working fast enough. I emailed the report updates. Detective Carin must stop the killer. The nurse is the killer.'* What does he mean you're *not working fast enough*?"

Shaking her head in the negative, Carin breathes and tries not to appear frustrated.

"Al thinks the killer is a woman who uses a nurse's uniform to hide in plain sight. I have no proof, nor does Al, that the killer is a woman."

"Forensics? DNA?"

"Our people down the hall and the state lab found nothing. Whoever is doing this is not dumb."

"I think I understand. There is another press conference tomorrow, and I haven't seen your notes for approval. What are you going to say?"

"Say? Nothing. I haven't had time to think about another press conference."

"Carin, the press is all over this, and you have to have something for them tomorrow."

"Give me an hour. You'll have my notes. I don't have

any suspects, and it doesn't look like the victims knew each other. There are a few people of interest. I've got nothing solid or actionable. I found no links other than the medical facility, Dr. Greene, and the McKinnon Funeral Home. Thanks, Chief. Anything else?"

"Yes. Al is my nephew. His mother, Deena, is my wife's cousin. Deena came into my wife's family after her mother remarried. It is a small community that was much smaller not too many years ago. Our parents moved to Marble Grove in the early sixties during the boom and still live across the street from each other."

The chief, Carin's boss, stops, smiles wide, and waits. Not knowing what else to ask, Carin plays it cool.

"I didn't know you were from Marble Grove."

"According to the old-timers, our families are still outsiders. Our parents were considered hippies who moved in with a passel of rowdy children. I came along after my parents moved here and was the youngest by a decade. Mom called me her miracle. My family resettled here from a broken-down farm in South Dakota. Deena's parents moved the family from somewhere in Louisiana, which was probably smart for a couple in a biracial marriage. Our families had no money. A hockey scholarship was my way out. I graduated high school and then left for college and a career. I came back because home is home. This is a good place to live. Even if half the force thinks one of their relatives should have been named chief. Back to the case, my nephew Al is no dummy."

Carin closes her mouth and decides to remain silent

about the inbred nature of rural communities and her boss knowing more than she imagined.

"Yep. I knew that would be new information. Detective Trimble, you missed a step."

"I did?"

"From now on, make sure you know everyone's history, and I mean *everyone*, who might have relevance to your investigation."

"Understood. So you know, I looked at Al's background. I didn't connect him to you. You probably know your nephew has never been arrested. There is nothing to indicate he is a troublemaker or looking for glory. He might want credit for helping. It's nothing serious to worry about."

"Good work. Don't worry about the hospital lawyers. They're just doing their job. You can leave."

* * *

Carin felt her first press conference was a disappointment. Today's press conference is another lesson in humility. The two reporters and the busybody are back, along with the camera streaming the session.

"That's all the new information. Yes, Mr. Wenderling."

"Call me Norv. Detective Trimble, do you have everything you need to solve the Nursing Home Murders?"

"Chief Johnston actively works to ensure the MGHDP has everything it needs to protect the citizens of Marble Grove and Hemingway County."

"I meant, doesn't the FBI usually take over cases where the suspect might be a serial killer?"

"Yes, that is true. Chief Johnston has requested assistance. At this time, we are researching all possible leads. That's it for today. When I know more, you will know more."

Chapter Nine

Case ID :	A-115
Name of Deceased :	Robert Maurice LeClare
Date of Report :	31-Aug-23
Cause of Death :	A gunshot in the heart
Place of Death :	165-B Barrow Lane
Date of Death :	30-Aug-23
Time of Death :	23:00-02:00
Investigator :	Marcus Alvin Demchuk

Background
The victim lives at home with hospice

Details
1) No bullet fragments at the scene.
2) No residents heard the gunshot.
3) No exit wounds.

Shooter retrieved the bullet from the victim.
Method of bullet retrieval: Unknown.
People known to visit Robert: None

"Sharon, did you hear the news?"

"No, Louie, what happened?"

"Another patient was murdered."

Waiting for her boss, Dr. Greene, to finish putting too much artificial creamer into her coffee, Louie feels the breakroom is closing in on the pair. Standing in the doorway, Louie is forcing her boss to ask.

"Who was murdered this time?"

"The radio report mentioned the police investigator was at the home of Robert LeClare — Tercia's brother, Bobby."

"So what? Bobby was responding to the pain medication. He had a few days, maybe a week, to live."

"So what? Come on, Sharon. Someone is killing our patients. Doesn't that make you nervous?"

"No. Does it make *you* nervous?"

"Why would I be nervous? Sharon, this is not normal. Is there something you want to tell me?"

"Lou, do you think I killed those patients? Maybe it was *you* who killed them."

Frustrated, tossing her cream-loaded coffee down the drain, rinsing the mug, and placing it upside down in the drying rack calms the doctor. Sharon looks up at her assistant, forcing herself to lighten her face and tone.

"I didn't kill anyone, and I know you are not a killer. I hope you are not a killer. Someone is murdering our patients and wants to pin it on us. Louie, I didn't do it. Let's get back to work."

Not believing the words she heard from the doctor, Louie watches her boss form a manufactured smile before heading down the hall to the day's first patient.

* * *

Walking the broken and heaving sidewalk toward the

bungalow-style house, Carin notices Barrow Lane does not, and probably never had, elm trees lining the sidewalks. Expensive trees go to those who pay the highest taxes, four blocks north and four blocks east — literally, the other side of the tracks.

A patrol officer, along with Mari and Ash, are all standing on the porch of number 165-B Barrow Lane, waiting for the detective to arrive. Reading Al's report on her phone, Carin looks up and accepts the officer opening the screen door for her.

The main living space is to the front door's left, and the formal dining room is to the right. Healthcare workers replaced the dining table and chairs with an articulated rolling bed. Staring, unblinking, the deceased Robert LeClare looks like he is sitting up.

Inside the bungalow, standing in a line between the rooms, Carin, Mari, and Ash review the scene. Ash is unable to remain quiet.

"What happened to his face?"

Feeling overwhelmed, Carin ignores the twenty-something's lack of self-control and compassion. Snapping on vinyl gloves before picking up and reading the chart that should not have been left on the sideboard, the detective speaks quietly. Wrinkling her nose at the necrotic smell of decay, the detective scans the chart while speaking.

"This was a nice home. Home healthcare left their notes. Malignant melanoma. I've done my homework. Cancer deaths per population are way down. Some cancers are still a death sentence. This is one of the worst. Never go out in the sun without sunscreen. Mari?"

"Carin, do we have another one?"

A patrol officer, whom Carin overlooked standing in the doorway, chirps.

"Another what?"

Looking at the name sewn onto the center of his body armor, just above his body camera, Carin gently chastises the new officer.

"Officer Zumbro, shouldn't you be outside, ensuring the neighbors aren't panicking?"

Zumbro leaves without a word, letting the screen door bang against the jamb. Carin turns back to Mari with a raised eyebrow and receives a question she did not expect.

"How long before the FBI shows up?"

"A few days. Ash, get on your phone, find out where the forensics team is, and get them here. Use my name."

Ash steps to the far edge of the living room to make the ordered call. Carin steps close to Mari, away from the medical and necrotic odors, and tries to ignore how good the first responder smells. All sources of information are good sources, and Mari sees a lot of accident victims and dead people. Carin whispers and receives the same.

"Mari, who is killing the terminal patients?"

"Someone with medical knowledge or access to medical records. A doctor or a nurse. These people were in their last days. Why kill someone about to die? This is not about the victims. This is about personal satisfaction. Someone thinks they're being a good Samaritan. The killer has convinced themselves they're acting with nobility in ending the pain of those suffering so badly."

Impressed with Mari's detailed observation, Carin enjoys Mari's perfume until Ash returns from across the room.

"Dispatch says forensics is ten minutes out."

"Thank you, Ash. Mari, you've been thinking about this case."

"Ash and I have a lot of time to talk. Where's your partner?"

"If you mean Al, I have no idea. I received his report via email. You know, that is a good question. He's usually poking around and knows too much about these murders. I'll have to check on him later. Right now, what do you think?"

Mari leans over the body, causing the newbie Ash to gag that his partner is so close to the disfigured face that is giving off a rancid odor. The senior EMT pulls the comforter away and peeks at the victim's chest.

"Carin, look, it is the same marks."

"Thanks. Wait for forensics, then take the body to Marc. I am going to canvas the neighborhood with the patrol officer."

"Who is Marc?"

Mari saves her partner before Carin can bite again at the newbie's naïve attitude.

"Marc Downsen is the coroner. An EMT should know that little piece of information. Get the gurney from the truck. Carin, have you looked into Jared McKinnon?"

"The guy who owns the funeral business?"

"No, Jared McKinnon Senior. Lots of funny stuff happened while he was the coroner. Might be worth a few minutes to look into his business while he was a county employee."

"I will. Thanks for the heads up."

Wanting to stay and enjoy Mari's presence, Carin reconsiders, smiles and exits the home. On the porch, Officer Zumbro looks at the small crowd of neighbors collecting on the sidewalk when Carin strolls by, issuing a soft order.

"Come with me."

Zumbro knows how to follow orders. Ash parts the crowd so he can come through with the gurney. Carin stops near the group with patrol officer Zumbro on her shoulder. Standing as tall as possible and looking serious, she turns toward one of the neighbors.

"I am Detective Carin Trimble. Your neighbor, Robert LeClare, has passed."

"We know who you are. Are you here because Bobby was murdered?"

"I know you. You were at the press conferences. What is your name?"

"I am Marg Lyttle. I live right there, 165-A."

Patrol officer Zumbro interrupts for his hand-written notes.

"How do you spell your name?"

"M-A-R-G, and it is pronounced Marj. L-Y-T-T-L-E, and it is Ly-ttle, not Little. Wyatt, you should know my name."

Marg Lyttle points at the house attached to the LeClare

house. Not wanting to err again, Carin confirms that the woman has no wedding ring.

"Miss Lyttle, I see your porch camera. We may need the video. Have you seen anything unusual?"

"The nurse came earlier than normal. Otherwise, no. How many people have been killed?"

"What makes you think Mr. LeClare was killed?"

"I heard the noise."

"What noise? Can you describe the sound?"

"Yeah, like in the movies when they push a pillow to someone's face and then shoot them dead through the pillow."

"I see. Television and movies are often inaccurate. Are you sure you remember it correctly?"

"I know what I heard. Why did the new nurse come so early?"

"How early?"

"Before the sun was up."

"Miss Lyttle, were you up before the sun?"

"Every day."

"The early arriving nurse, did you see her face?"

"His face and no."

"The nurse was a man?"

"I think so. A white man. He had on scrubs and a black hoodie pulled tight."

"How do you know he was white?

"I saw his hands."

"He wore scrubs? His pants were scrubs?"

"Yes, and a black hoodie."

"If you didn't see the person's face, what makes you think it was a man?"

"He walked like a man."

Realizing Marg Lyttle is a busybody who watches too many crime dramas, Carin changes tactics.

"Did anyone else see or hear anything?"

A few people in the small crowd mutter no or shake their heads. Marg Lyttle always has something more to say.

"He was about your height. Maybe shorter. Not as tall as you and skinnier. He walked with a purpose."

Ignoring Marg's veiled insult about her weight, Carin turns to Officer Zumbro, waves him forward, and then scans the crowd for details before closing the discussion without looking at Marg.

"Officer Zumbro will take your names and any statement you want to make. If you think of anything after speaking to Officer Zumbro, call the police and ask for me. Use the non-emergency number, not 911."

The forensics team pulls to a stop, and Carin waves for them to follow her into the house. Carin knows she will lose control of the case in a day, maybe two, when the FBI arrives. Her phone chirps as Mari and Ash join her in the cozy living room.

Stepping away and listening to a one-sided conversation, the group watches Carin's face grow pale.

"I have to go. Mari, Ash, when the forensic people are finished, take the body to Marc."

Rushing, Carin nearly collides face-first with patrol officer Zumbro.

"Officer, keep this to yourself. Create your reports. Do not speak to anyone about what you saw here."

"Call me Wyatt. Speak to anyone? Who would I speak to?"

"The press. If the press asks, you know nothing."

Carin rushes to her car, buckles in, and notices Marg Lyttle's ever-watchful eye is on her.

Chapter Ten

Arriving at the correct room, Carin's mother is asleep. Not waiting to wake Mom, Carin realizes she is tired and decides to stay, using the upholstered chair. The recliner is comfy after finding the handle between the cushion and the arm and raising the footrest.

Carin wakes up covered in a blanket that was not there when she fell asleep. A familiar voice yanks the detective into reality.

"You are awake. Finally. How long have you been here?"

Throwing off the cover, standing, and stretching before moving to the bed, Carin holds her mother's hand and fights back the tears. The idea of her vibrant mother lying in a hospital bed is overwhelming to the detective.

"Mom, what are *you* doing here? The nurses told me you have been here a week."

"It has been a couple of days. Cari, how long have you been here?"

"I got here yesterday afternoon. When the nurse called, I came right over. You were sedated. The nurses told me to come back. I waited. I wanted to be here when you woke up. I guess I was tired."

"You stayed overnight? What time is it? Is that the sun coming up? Did you see the nurse poke her head in and then leave?"

Surprised she slept through the night, wanting desperately to pee, Carin looks around, collects herself, and responds to her mother.

"No, I did not see anyone. Why?"

"It seemed odd. The nurse stepped in, looked at you, and mumbled that she'd give us privacy before she turned around and left. *What am I doing here?* Cari, is that the best question a police detective should ask? I woke up about an hour ago and waited for you to wake up. You look tired. Are you sleeping?"

Carin takes a moment to remember the instructions she received to deal with stressful moments. Her mother, Claudia Marani Trimble, is fun-loving and adventurous, and being in a hospital bed is another opportunity to be snarky. Carin knows her too well. As she prefers to be called, Claudie does not allow any conversation to be easy or light. To Claudie, every moment is an opportunity to learn. Carin returns from the small bathroom to a smiling Claudie.

"You're always the same. You talk to anyone about anything, and here I am — confused, worried, and not knowing what is happening with you. Mother, how come you didn't tell me you have cancer? What kind of cancer?"

"Breast cancer. Metastasized breast cancer. I didn't tell you because it was no big deal."

"I am not surprised you didn't tell me. You can be stubborn. Why ask anyone for help? Right? Don't answer. What changed? Why did you have the nurse call me?"

"It was no big deal. Now. Well…"

"What do you mean? Mom, help me understand."

"I mean, I have a few weeks, maybe a couple of months."

"Mom?"

"The doctors in Amarillo sent me to Denver. The people at the Rocky Mountain facility were terrific. Sometimes, even the best have nothing left to offer. That's it. I accept it. Cari, you should, too."

Carin knows her mother is not herself and presses the conversation soothingly, hiding the fear of losing her mother.

"Why here, at this hospital? Why not a facility closer to home, Amarillo, Dallas, or Denver? Where is Dad?"

"Dad's taking care of the farm. You know that, too. Why are you asking questions to which you know the answers? That's not like you. Is it the new case?"

"Does Dad know about the cancer?"

"Of course, he knows. Who do you think drove me all the way up here? The Nguyen boys took care of the farm while your father was away. What a nice family. Before you ask, I told your father not to call you. Cari, honey, what is wrong with you?"

"Mom, this is a shock. How did I not know?"

"What else? I know you. Cari, something is happening that is affecting how you think."

"How did you talk Dad into letting you stay here, alone, for the treatment?"

"Your father knows what's happening to me. He and I had long discussions, and we agreed to the plan. If it works, great. If it fails, you know your father. He doesn't want to be here if the treatment is unsuccessful. If I make it, I'll go home. If I don't, you'll take care of me."

Shocked at her mother's pragmatic approach, the only

child realizes she shouldn't be surprised. She knows Claudia Trimble is a firebrand who devours information and is always willing to give an opinion. Sure that her mother has bullied her father into accepting the diagnosis, Carin waits.

"Tell me what is bugging my favorite daughter."

"I'm your only daughter."

"As far as you know."

"Whatever. You're constantly throwing out ideas about ulterior motives. You have always been fond of creating your version of reality. I'm not buying it. Now you are here, and I have my first big case, and I don't know how to solve it. They are going to have to take it away."

After a pause to collect her thoughts, Carin is mildly surprised her mother has not filled the silence with a question.

"I am sorry. Mom, this time is about you. Is it a coincidence you are here? Something tells me I need to know more about your diagnosis and treatment plan. Sorry. This is about you. What can I do to help you?"

"Take it away? What does that mean?"

"It means my boss, the chief, will call in the FBI."

Not wanting to fib to her mother, Carin corrects herself.

"He already made the call. They'll be here tomorrow."

"Oh. Well. That is not good. Is it bad?"

"It's not good or bad. It's good to get help when you need it. It's bad that I'll be taken off as the lead investigator."

"Will you still be involved in the case?"

"Yes. In a support role. Maybe."

"I see. Cari, what will you do before the FBI shows up?"

"That's the thing. I don't know what to do next. Wait. Back up. Mother, why are you here, in this hospital?"

"Dr. Greene."

"Dr. Greene? Mom, have you received a second opinion?"

"Several, actually. They all have the same story and sing the same song. Chemo. Radiation. Diet. Hope. No one could promise to stop the pain. That's how I ended up here."

"Do you mean in Dr. Greene's pain trial?

"Yes. Sharon has new ideas about treating stage IV cancers. She has helped me with the pain and other symptoms."

"Pain management. Not a cure? Is surgery an option? Chemo? Mother, help me understand."

"They call it palliative care. It is special care for people with serious illnesses. Palliative care focuses on providing relief. It's a tool to ease the symptoms and stress of having cancer. They use it for other diseases, too. I think. Anyway, the goal is a better quality of life for both the patient and the family. No more surgery. No more chemo. No more radiation."

"No more surgery? What? You came here to die? Stop the pain and die? Mother, damn it!"

"When you were stationed in Germany, I had a double mastectomy."

Breathing, using her techniques to cope with stress, and visualizing pleasant thoughts, Carin does what she has been doing since she was a teen. Accepting her mother's oddities is a simple coping mechanism. Using one of the processes she learned in counseling, Carin pushed her rising anxiety into a mental corner before speaking in a soothing and civil tone.

"I was only in Germany for a few months. They call it TDY — Temporary Duty. If you were diagnosed then — you've had cancer all this time, and you didn't tell me?"

"I was in remission after the surgery. The chemo and radiation didn't work, and the cancer came back. Now it's in my brain and my lungs."

Stunned and confused, Carin steps to the window and finds birds flittering in the trees. Al would know what kind of birds she sees. The idea that her partner would know the birds by their sound makes her smile a little, despite the bomb her mother has just dropped. A minor epiphany settles on Carin's mind. Her mother here, in Marble Grove, cannot be a coincidence. Carin's attention is pulled back into the room when PA Mancone arrives.

"Hello, Detective Trimble. Hello, Claudia."

Carin watches the woman she admires talk to the PA and knows her mother is fighting the pain. Carin watches in mild surprise as her mother returns to her nature. Cantankerously funny is how people think of Claudie Trimble.

"Hello, Louie. I told you, call me Claudie. Everyone does."

"Claudie, how are you feeling today?"

"Since they opened that valve on that I-V tube, I feel great. Thank you, sir. May I have some more?"

In awe at her mother's relaxed attitude and knowing

the vibrant woman is holding back, Carin watches the unfolding interaction with the PA. With an eye on her mother's face, Carin forces herself to stay quiet.

"Funny. Claudie, any more of that juice, and you'd be flying."

"I am already flying. This is my daughter, Carin."

"We've met."

Carin catches Louie's crisp tone when admitting to having met previously.

"You met my daughter? I see. No grandkids for me. You make sure Cari picks up the tab."

"It's, not like that. I'm married. Detective Trimble had a few medical questions about a case she was working. I see you're feeling okay. I'll return with Dr. Greene tomorrow morning, around 10:00. We'll discuss your treatment plan with Dr. Greene. Claudie. Detective."

Louie is barely out of the room when Claudie rolls her head toward her daughter with a gleam in her eye.

"You need to find a girl like that. Or a nice man."

"Yes, Mother."

Rolling her eyes, leaning in for a hug, Carin says goodbye — hoping it is not the last goodbye.

"I have to go home, shower, and check in at work. Then, I'll be back this afternoon and tomorrow for Dr. Greene's visit. Is that okay?"

"Sure. Cari?"

"Yes, Mom?"

"You can solve the case."

Unable to respond to her mother's unfounded

confidence, Carin leaves the room.

* * *
** ** **

She watched the microwave count down on another pre-packaged pile of pastry-wrapped mush growing too hot. Carin was awake when her cell phone chirped with a text message before 6:00. Not bothering to answer the text with a text, she reasoned Marc must be up for a call.

"Marc, it's six in the morning. You're up early. Are you at work?"

"Yes. I couldn't sleep. Something about the body was bugging me. I was right."

"Right, about what? What are you saying?"

"I am saying he was dead before he was shot in the heart. Someone shot him because they could."

"Or the gunshot is an attempt to disguise something else. Do you have the pathology for the victims? Marc, I may need some information. Can you run a few tests?"

"I have pathology for the recent cases. What do you want me to look for in the samples?"

"Look for anything unusual. Maybe the gunshots are a diversion."

"Diversion? Oh. Wait, what? Oh! Someone is trying to hide why they died. I'm on it."

"Thanks, Marc."

Deena Demchuk is filling the doorway. Behind the screen door, the overprotective mother blocks the entry with one hand on her hip and the other hand on the door handle.

"Hello. I am Detective Trimble. I am looking for Albert, Al, Demchuk."

"I know who you are. Everyone knows the detective on the serial killer case. Al is my son. What do you want?"

"Al and I have been exchanging notes. I'd like to chat with him about the latest report he sent to me."

"The detective who knows nothing wants to take credit for Al's work."

Chapter Eleven

Carin was not expecting to have Mrs. Demchuk snap at her. She stands her ground and raises her shoulders. The screen door is a barrier. Barrier or not, the detective is ready to argue. Luckily, John Demchuk approaches and gently touches his wife's shoulder to prevent the argument from erupting.

"Come in, Detective. I'll take you to Al."

Under the scowl of a devoted mother, Carin follows Al's father into the house, through the kitchen, past the breakfast nook, and down the slope. The trees surrounding the Demchuk home are dripping with bird feeders. The cacophony of bird sounds is overwhelming. The short journey ends at the front door of Al's apartment. Carin's new partner greets his father and the detective by blocking the door.

"She can't be here."

"She can. If you want to help with the case, you must let Detective Trimble into your office."

"But."

"No buts, Al."

Flustered, rubbing and flapping his hands, Al is one twitch away from a full-blown panic attack. Carin leans forward with a technique she read about in a pamphlet the Pritchett facility provided.

"Al, it's okay. I'll step back and wait on the sidewalk. It's a nice day. We can chat right here."

When Carin leans away and steps back, Al relaxes. After

a moment, Al nods and gives an almost imperceptible smile. Dad steps behind Carin, impressed the detective stopped Al before the meltdown became full-sized. Carin confirms Mom's nasty glare from the kitchen window before opening the conversation. John tries to answer for his wife's behavior.

"Don't worry about Deena. She's protective of Al."

Carin nods, knowing it is not the first time John has apologized for his wife. Firming her spine, the detective begins the questions.

"Al, I need to know how you access the medical files."

"It is a secret."

"I know it is a secret. Partners share secrets. It will help our case if you tell me how you access the medical records."

Al refuses to look at his father. Mr. Demchuk notices Al looking at Carin and comments.

"Detective Trimble, you've made a lot of progress with my son."

Accepting the compliment with a head rock and a smile, Carin returns to speaking with Al.

"*Partner*, it will help our case if you give me the details of how you access the medical records."

Eventually, Al points to his father. After a moment of confusion, Carin understands.

"I agree. Your father doesn't have clearance."

Dad takes the hint and heads slowly to the house under the frown of his disapproving wife, who is in the kitchen window.

"Okay, Partner, tell me how you gained access to the

medical records."

"Email on-the-line."

"You use email to access the medical records? How does your access to the email work?"

"No."

"No? You receive emails with the medical information?"

"Yes. No."

"Yes, you receive emails. No, the emails don't have medical information. Al, I am confused."

"Correlated."

Al looks away again, catching Carin off guard.

"What is correlated? Al, look at me. You can look at me, and I will tell you if it makes me uncomfortable. *Partner*, what is correlated?"

Al makes eye contact and then reverts to looking anywhere that is not Carin.

"The emails are correlated with the medical access."

"I see. The emails connect you to the medical information. Al, correlated can mean connected. Not in this way. Someone is sending you information. How are the emails connected to the medical records?"

Al looks again at Carin, then away, finds a bird, and listens for a moment before stepping into his office, leaving the door ajar. Carin steps through the door and into a mild surprise. Although Al calls it his office, it is a mother-in-law's apartment, and the room is immaculate.

Organized and tidy, the room is set up like a studio apartment with a bed to the left, a bathroom beyond the bed, and a small sofa facing a big-screen television to the right. Between everything, at the center of the back wall, under a large window, is a desk and Al's computer. Carin admires the trees and birds feeding through the window. Up the path, through the trees, an image destroys the idyllic view. Deena Demchuk stands at the kitchen sink, scowling and watching Carin and her son.

"Al, this is a nice room."

"It is my office."

"It's a nice office. Do you mind if I sit?"

Al bobs his head in a quick nod of affirmation, allowing Carin to sit on the arm of the sofa.

"Tell me about the emails. When did they start? How often do you receive them? Do you know who sends the information to you? Can you show me the emails?"

Al stops wringing his hands — he is happy Detective Carin finally calls on him for action. He signs into his computer. Watching the screen, Carin is amazed when Al's fingers fly over the keyboard. Leaning forward from the sofa's edge, Carin cannot read the email. She gives Al a confidence boost in a truthful comment.

"You type well."

"I learned."

"I see that. Is that the first email?"

"Yes. See?"

Squinting, Carin catches the first few lines of the email.

"Al, that email, is it dated a few months ago?"

"Yes."

"Some of the deaths in your files occurred before the

date of the email. May I step closer to read it?"

Al nods again, allowing Carin to step up close to her partner. Ordinarily wary of people being too close, especially from behind, the detective notices Al is unusually calm. Carin knows she is making progress.

"Show me each email. In order, if you can."

Al opens email after email, eight total, without a word, switching to the next when Carin nods or grunts after reading the previous message. None of the messages are more than two lines. Most are a single sentence with the name and location of the victim.

"The emails are all from someone who signed them: *Your Friend Sami.* Do you know anyone named Sami?"

"No."

"Have you replied to Sami?"

Al waves his head back and forth in the negative.

"Why not send a reply and try to talk to the person sending you the information?"

"I'm afraid."

Moving quickly away from her new friend's admission, Carin gives Al the bad news.

"That email address is a free account. It will be hard to trace. Partner, I have to tell you something."

"The FBI is coming."

"Yes. How did you know?"

"The FBI always happens on the TV."

"Yes, in the movies and television shows, the FBI or a special agency takes over significant cases. Our case is too big for one detective."

"Two."

"Sorry, our case is too big for two new detectives. Al, let's go through the emails again. Start at the beginning and tell me what you did every time you received an email."

An hour of reviewing the emails is enough time for Mrs. Demchuk to brew a pot of coffee, heat some cocoa, and zap a few brunch muffins. Marching into Al's office and placing the tray on the low table, Deena refuses to look at the detective.

"Al, be nice to your guest. Here is your hot chocolate and muffin. Today is not a porridge day."

"Coffee."

"Yes, Al, I made coffee for Detective Trimble."

"Thank you, Mrs. Demchuk."

Deena marches away without a word of kindness for the detective. Sipping coffee and letting Al eat a muffin, Carin notices John Demchuk watching from the kitchen. Satisfied that his wife has not picked a fight, John disappears when Deena opens the glass slider leading to the kitchen.

"Al, the FBI is probably going to take your computer. The information about the emails will help them find a link to the killer."

Al doesn't react, shocking Carin.

"You don't seem upset at the possibility the FBI will take your computer. Al, is there something you want me to see or something you want to tell me?"

"One more."

"One more what?"

"Email."

"Show me."

Hesitant to expose the contents, Al opens the email.

"It's from Laura. She is asking you for a date. Congrats."

Carin pauses when Al does not respond.

"I think congrats is right. Does Laura asking you for a date make you happy?"

"Yes. Maybe. No."

"Have you ever been on a date?"

Al does his negative shoulders and head shake.

"I see. Do you want some help?"

"Partner."

"Yes, we are partners. Partners help each other. I'll help you. First, this email is three days old. Laura probably thinks you are ghosting her. If you want a date with Laura, you should reply."

"Ghost?"

"Ghosting means ending a relationship without telling the other person. You should reply ASAP."

"A-S-A-P. As soon as possible. Now."

"You are correct. ASAP usually means now. Do you want me to help you write a response?"

Carin spends thirty precious minutes convincing Al that an early afternoon date at the café is perfect for a first date. Carin remembers that Laura is non-verbal when Al adds a reminder to the email for Laura to bring her phone. Appreciating her partner's willingness to open up to something new, the detective returns to the moment and the case.

"Al, when the FBI arrives, I will still be involved. It will be their case to manage. They will ask you a lot of questions. I want you to tell me you understand that they will come for your computer and ask you questions."

"A lot of questions. FBI will take the computer."

"Good. Thank you. I will talk to my chief, your uncle, later today. I'll text you an update if I have new information. Thank you for helping me with the emails. It's good information."

"Should I wear the blue shirt?"

Mildly concerned about Al changing the subject, Carin quickly understands.

"For the date? Yes, the blue shirt, the one with a collar, is nice. Not a T-shirt. Okay?"

"No T-shirt."

* * *

"Hello, Mom."

"Cari, you came."

"I told you I would be here for Dr. Greene's visit."

"You did? I don't remember. Is Dr. Greene the one who is helping me with the pain?"

Carin hides her shock at how much her mother's mental ability has deteriorated overnight.

"Mom, yesterday Dr. Greene was unable to make rounds. The nurse told me Dr. Greene will see you in a few minutes. Are you comfortable?"

"Yes, I'm fine. How did you know?"

"The nurse called me a couple of days ago. You told her to contact me. Mom, what can I do to help you feel better?"

"Better? Cari, I'm not getting better."

Fighting back the tears, Carin waits. Claudia Trimble has a moment of clarity.

"Cari, your father will not show his pain when I pass. Promise me you will help him."

"I promise. Hello, Dr. Greene. PA Mancone."

Carin turns and nods to the doctor and the PA and then steps back from the bed. Sharon Greene approaches Claudia from one side of the bed and Mancone on the other.

"Claudie, how are you feeling?"

"I'm okay, Dr. Greene."

"I told you, call me Sharon. I think you are fibbing. How is the pain?"

"No pain."

Claudie turns away her eyes from Dr. Greene, and they land on PA Mancone.

"Hello. You're new."

Ignoring the factual error, Louie smiles brightly in response to Claudie's confusion.

"Hello, Claudie. I'm Dr. Greene's assistant. Call me Louie."

"Hello, Louie. Cari, meet my team."

"Mom, I've met Dr. Greene and Mrs. Mancone. They are excellent. You will be feeling better soon."

Louie smiles at Carin, the sad tension becoming overwhelming. Dr. Greene's nod is nearly imperceptible, and she refuses to look at the detective. Carin and her mother lock eyes until Claudie speaks, barely above a whisper.

"How long?"

Greene looks at Louie before responding in a soft voice.

"Soon. Are you sure you feel okay?"

"No pain."

Carin's mother's eyes land on Louie again.

"Hello. You are new."

The pain and anguish are overwhelming, forcing Carin to draw in a deep breath before speaking.

"Mom, I'm going to wait in the hall. When Dr. Greene finishes, I'll come back. Is that okay?"

"Sure."

* * *
** ** **

The hallway is wide and immaculate, yet Carin feels the walls are closing in and will crush her any second. After several minutes, Greene stops with Louie. Both wear a forced smile before Greene speaks.

"Detective Trimble."

"Carin."

"Carin, your mother has a few hours. Fortunately, the pain is being managed. Is there anything I can do for you?"

"No, thank you. Dr. Greene, I know why you didn't tell me you were treating my mother. Rules and regulations are important. Knowing my mother was dying from cancer superseded rules and regulations. Minimally, you should have told me to speak to my mother. I'd have had more time with her if you had told me something. Anything."

"I can't agree with you. Yes, sometimes, there are exceptions. Breaking patient confidentiality is not something I can accept."

"Can't accept? That's callous."

"Maybe. Carin, your mother instructed us not to tell you anything. She was adamant that you not be told about her condition."

Louie steps slightly forward to interject and soften Greene's tone.

"Even if you had asked, we would not have admitted to anything. Carin, your mother didn't want anything to get in the way of your recent promotion. She was, is, proud of you."

Not knowing what to say, Carin walks away.

*** *** ***

In the parking lot, under the shade of a young elm, Carin calls her father.

"Hello, Dad. Please turn off the tractor. I'm glad you carry your cell phone with you now."

Darryl Lee Trimble waits for the noise to end before he responds to his only daughter.

"Hello, Cari. Is this about your mother? Has she passed?"

"No. It will be soon. I spoke to the doctor. There's nothing more they can do for Mom. Dad, shouldn't you be here with Mom and me?"

"Cari, your mother, and I planned for this day. She knew

it would come soon. Long before the doctors, she knew it would be soon. How are you? How is the big case?"

"I'm fine, thank you for asking. Dad, how do you know about the case?"

"I read."

"Read what?"

"Your local newspaper is online. They are not saying nice things about you."

"About me? Dad, I don't know what you're talking about."

"I heard the detective you replaced was interviewed. He rambled about you being too young to solve the case. The hint was he didn't think a woman should be a detective."

"Dad, I'm not surprised. Lots of people are stuck in the fifties. It doesn't matter. The FBI will be here today or tomorrow. I'll be pushed into the corner when the Feds show up."

"I'm sorry, Cari. It doesn't mean you're not a good detective."

"Dad, what about Mom?"

"The McKinnon Funeral Home will take care of the body."

"The McKinnon Funeral Home?"

"Yes, they gave a discount for prepayment. Your mom agreed and saved a lot of money. They will transport your mother for burial here, next to your grandparents."

Carin realizes her father's matter-of-fact tone and attitude result from his long conversations with her overly pragmatic mother. Pushing aside Jared McKinnon's name being attached to her family's private business, Carin practically begs her father for information.

"Dad, I know this is Mom's doing and not yours. It feels like this is just another day to you."

Choking out the words, Darryl ends the discussion.

"Cari, it is another day. That is how it works for me. Anything else, and nothing would get done. I love you, Cari."

"I love you, Dad."

Carin is sure her father disconnected the phone, and his pain, before he heard the word, *Dad*. Breathing deeply, remembering her training and therapy sessions, Carin knows she has to lock away the pain. Push it down and lock it away until the investigation ends.

Chapter Twelve

"Hello, Chief Johnston, Detective Trimble. I am Special Agent Karim Mojtabai. Call me Mosh."

Indian or Middle Eastern by heritage and born in Virginia, Karim Mojtabai has a perpetual smile. Chief Johnston waves a hand as if shooing away Mosh's formality.

"Call me Al."

"Thank you for allowing us to use your conference room. Detective Trimble, the chief filed a request for assistance. Why don't you tell me what you have so far, and we'll create a plan."

"Call me Carin. Chief, do you want us to move to another conference room?"

"No need. You can use this room. I'll sit in and observe."

"Okay, Chief. Mosh, what do you want to know?"

"Carin, start at the beginning."

"The coroner, Marc Downsen, will be here at ten. I'll run down the timeline, we'll review Marc's report, and then take a break for lunch. Chief, I'd like to visit my mother at lunch."

"That will be fine. Does noon to two work?"

"Yes, Chief. Mosh?"

"Fine by me."

"I am sorry."

"Dr. Greene, I'm sure you did everything possible. I have a question."

They are looking at the deceased Claudia Trimble. Greene and Trimble are about to face off, and each knows the tension is about to rise.

"You want to know about the pain. You want to understand why some people, like your mother, respond well to the pain management medications and others do not."

"Something like that."

"Exactly like that. The answer is we don't know. There are lots of theories. The truth is a mystery. We form intelligent conclusions about known factors. Your mother was a lucky one. The pain meds worked well for her up to the end. She died peacefully."

Carin retains a stoic face, accepting her mother's pain was managed until the end. The PTSD training is racing through her mind and keeping her from losing it at the loss of her mother. She knows Greene has prepped her response. Convinced the doctor is hiding information, the detective uses a softer tone.

"Dr. Greene, why would someone kill people who were dying? Why kill people who had hours or days remaining to live?"

Greene responds with a pitch dialed down from her typically tart voice.

"First, be assured that your mother died peacefully and without pain. How would I know the answer to that? Isn't it your job to find the killer and ask them?"

Greene sniping back, albeit in a soft voice, adds another positive layer to Carin's suspicions. The new detective is convinced Greene is the murderer, or, at least, knows who is killing the people with late-stage cancer and unmanageable pain.

"I spoke to my father. The arrangements are complete. Thank you for all your work, Dr. Greene."

Spinning on her heel and leaving without a word, the anguish refuses to stay locked away. Carin considers whether a stiff drink is needed.

"There are three bars in town and the roadhouse out on the route. Which one will have the fewest people? People. As soon as I step inside, the town will know. Do I want to give up everything? All the sessions. All the talking to understand what happened in the desert. Alcohol does not fix pain. Alcohol is a crutch. Living a good life is healing enough."

Stiffening her spine and deciding not to drink, she drives to the café where she and Al discussed the case. At the outside table, watching people strolling the sidewalk, Carin is sure half of the pedestrians are staring at the failed detective.

A child of about ten, walking with her mother, stops and gives Carin a note. The youngster giggles before looking up at her mother, whose face Carin knows. Trying to remember, she cannot place the woman's face. Before the mother and child are too far away, it dawns on Carin that she knows the mother and hollers at the backsides of the woman and girl.

"Laura?"

The child returns an over-the-shoulder smile. The mother does not react to Carin's shout. Looking at the paper in her hand, unfolding the small scrap, the message reads: *Find the Booger.*

Ignoring the child's prank, Carin decides the investigation, and her career as a detective is over before she solves her first case.

** ** **

"That is all good information. Chief, your detective has done a stellar job. I read the case files and am aware of your nephew's involvement. I am unsure what more I would have done in her place."

"Thank you, that means a lot. I'm going to step out. Duty calls."

"Thanks, Chief. I'll let you know if Carin and I come up with anything."

Carin and Mojtabai wait for the conference room door to close.

"Carin, use the whiteboard. Let's run down your suspects."

Jared McKinnon

"Jared McKinnon, Jr., is the owner of the McKinnon Funeral Home and Mortuary. The pandemic was good for the funeral business. The sales slump has hit the funeral business hard. Also, I looked into the industry. Cremation is preferred, cheaper, and doesn't bring in the high-margin profit that comes with a single-use coffin. My guess is he's trying to keep a desperate business in operation. I have not yet subpoenaed his business records."

"Carin, why kill people just to get paid sooner? Most of the victims would have died in a few days or weeks. It seems like a stretch to go to all the trouble of murder when the money will come your way soon."

"I agree. Jared McKinnon is a common thread to many of the deaths on the list."

"Okay, Detective, go on."

Jared McKinnon
Dr. Sharon Greene

"Greene is common to seven of the thirteen victims. We'll need a warrant for the patients' background information. The doctor is worth further discussion."

"I can see from the reports and your notes you don't like Dr. Greene."

"Like or dislike is not relevant. Greene is testy about her patients. I think — this is just an opinion — I believe Greene is disappointed in the results of the pain study she leads."

"Tell me more."

"What if Greene knows the pain meds are failing and wants to stop her patients from suffering?"

"I can see that is a possibility. A warrant, it is. Next."

Jared McKinnon
Dr. Sharon Greene
Lauren Mancone

"Mancone is Greene's PA. She knows all the patients."

"What about Lauren? Is she a source of background information?"

"More than that. Lauren is called Louie, and how she acts around Greene is odd. Again, it is a vibe I got when I first spoke to Greene and Mancone. Louie gave me a negative head shake behind Greene's back. We can get information about Greene and the pain study from Mancone."

"Another good thought. We'll tack Mancone onto the warrant. You've done everything right so far. What have you missed? What about the chief? Put his name up there."

Reluctant, Carin writes on the whiteboard.

Jared McKinnon
Dr. Sharon Greene
Lauren Mancone
Chief Johnston

"And? Detective Trimble, what are you missing? Are you being pointed in the wrong direction?"

"You are suggesting the chief is pointing me away from something."

"Not exactly."

Standing, marker in hand, Carin accepts Mosh's request to assess her boss's possible role in the investigation.

"The chief doesn't say much — he leaves me to do my job. I don't know what he doesn't want me to find. If anything. If I think it is necessary to investigate, he lets me investigate."

Thinking and talking to herself, Carin verbalizes her confusion.

"Wait a minute. I wonder. That makes no sense. Why would the chief impede an investigation?"

Carin realizes she is talking in circles and wipes the chief from the whiteboard before continuing the discussion with the federal agent.

"Why would the chief misdirect?"

"I don't know. I gleaned the idea from your notes about the chief being the uncle of your informant."

"I never thought of the chief's nephew Al as an informant."

"Who else have you not written on the board? Carin, you are forgetting the center of this investigation. Never forget to always start with the family. You forgot, or are avoiding, the chief's nephew. Your partner."

Carin knows Mojtabai is correct and replaces the chief's name on the whiteboard.

Jared McKinnon

Dr. Sharon Greene

Lauren Mancone

Marcus Alvin Demchuk

"I guess something in my subconscious doesn't want it to be true. Al knows way too much about the murders. I don't think my new *'partner'* is the murderer. He might be an accomplice. Unlikely. Maybe."

"That's the best detective work I saw in your reports. However, you have not followed through. Just because you don't want it to be true doesn't make it inaccurate. What are we going to do next?"

"Next? I have no clue. Isn't that why you're here?"

"Sort of. Your forensics people didn't find any unaccounted-for DNA. I requested Marc Downsen send the pathology to our lab in Virginia. Maybe our lab can pull some DNA. We'll know in a couple of days if there is anything unusual. I suspect they will find loads of whatever pain meds Greene pushes. We wait for the warrant, then talk to Greene and Mancone."

"Agreed. What should I do while we wait?"

Interrupted by a commotion outside the conference room, Carin quickly erases the whiteboard and follows Mosh into the cubicle farm.

At the far end of the open space, Al is flailing and turning in circles. Uniformed officers are standing in a circle around the panicked visitor. Carin rushes forward into the ring of officers with her arms wide as if moving in for a hug, palms visible.

"Al, stop. Look at me, Al!"

Al stops and smiles at his partner. Carin immediately knows he has put on a show.

"Al, what happened?"

"They said I couldn't see you. I have a report. They said I had to leave."

While silently pushing the officers back with her open palms, Carin guesses correctly.

"Al, this is Special Agent Mojtabai. Do you want to talk with the special agent and me?"

"Yes."

*** *** ***

"I know you, and you need to relax. It is just a conference room. Al, lots of rooms don't have windows."

"There are no trees."

"I know you like windows and being able to see outside. Al, you have to calm down. I know you made up the tantrum in the foyer because they told you to wait or come back. I am on to you and your ways."

"Yes."

"Yes, what? Help me understand."

"Yes, they would not let me see you. I have information for you and the special agent."

Three heads turn to the door opening.

"Hello, Uncle Myron."

"Hello, Al. My team tells me you created a problem."

"I have information for Detective Carin and Special Agent."

"Al, call me Mosh."

"I have information for Detective Carin and Special

133

Agent Mosh."

"That's good news. Please give the detectives the information and then go home. I need you to promise me you will go straight home."

"Don't tell Mom."

"Al, I know you well enough to know you are upsetting your mother, and you know it. Go home. Have a nice dinner."

"I have information."

"Al, what did I do when you were little and wouldn't listen?"

"You picked me up."

"Do you want me to do that again? I can. You're not that big."

Al smiles at the memories of his uncle. Carin and Mojtabai watch the caring uncle's interaction with his nephew.

"I will go home. Don't tell Mom."

"Okay, Al. Give the detectives the information and head straight home. I'll be in the next room if you need anything."

Mojtabai leans his head toward Carin, allowing her to begin talking with Al.

"You mentioned you have information. Can we see the information?"

"I want a dog."

Carin looks at Mosh, shrugs, then asks.

"A dog?"

"Yes, a dog. Canis lupus familiaris. Maybe a Basenji.

Basenjis are small and smart, and they don't bark. Mother will let me have a dog that does not bark."

Mojtabai raises an eyebrow at Carin, who presses forward.

"Why do you want to get a dog?"

"I can take it on walks. If I have a dog, people will not be afraid of me when I walk. I don't walk because people stare at me. If I walk with a dog, people will be nice."

"I'm sorry people aren't friendly. Dogs are a lot of work and need a lot of care. Maybe a dog isn't the answer. When this is over, we can take walks together."

Mojtabai instinctively knows to remain quiet and lets Carin continue to pull the information from Al.

"You are being nice, Detective Carin. We can walk. You are busy. I am going to get a dog and name it Booger."

Flabbergasted, Carin is almost too soft to hear.

"Booger? Al, where did you get the idea for that name?"

"It is in my report."

"Al, you have given me a dozen reports. Which report?"

"I have not given you the report."

"Al, Partner, where did you get the name Booger?"

"The Nurse-Doctor has a dog named Booger."

"The Nurse-Doctor? Do you mean Lauren Mancone?"

"Louie."

Carin eyes Mojtabai and then returns to Al when Mosh asks.

"Al, who is Louie?"

"Nurse Louie is a doctor on the weekend." Al has answered without answering, and Carin understands.

Mojtabai raises an eyebrow in confusion.

"Do you have your report?"

"No."

Carin leans gently in to help.

"Partner, I think you are deliberately confusing us. What are you trying to tell me?"

Al looks at Mojtabai and then back at the table. Carin presses the nervous Al.

"Special Agent Mosh is on the case now. He is our new partner. You know partners share secrets."

When Al refuses to speak, Carin hits on an idea.

"Investigator Demchuk, you are ordered to report your findings."

Chapter Thirteen

Mojtabai raises the other eyebrow yet remains silent. Carin shuffles, waiting for Al to reach a calm place.

"Nurse-Doctor Louie is the killer."

"That is an accusation that has no supporting evidence. Where is the report you came here to give to me? Is the report in your backpack?"

"No report. Verbal."

"Do you mean you are giving us the report verbally?"

"Yes. Verbal."

"Well. Tell us how you decided Lauren Mancone is shooting people."

"Claudia Trimble."

Stunned that Al has spoken her mother's name, Carin falls on her training and breathes deeply before asking.

"Did you get an email about my mother? Was my mother next?"

"Email."

The small conference room is closing in on Carin.

"What is in the email? Did you send it to me? Please send it to me."

Mojtabai leans forward, catching Carin's attention, and increases his smile as he speaks to Al in a comforting manner.

"Can you tell us what is in the email that references Detective Carin's mother?"

"Same as the others. Claudia Trimble died."

"I think I understand. You received the email. You

prepared the report. Claudia Trimble died before you could convey the information to Detective Carin."

"It is correlated correctly."

Mojtabai looks at Carin with a twisted face, and she takes the hint.

"You were sad for me and didn't want to upset me with a report about my mother."

Al rocks his body in agreement. The walls feel less constraining, and Carin quietly helps her friend.

"It's okay, Al. Thank you for being kind to me. Let's go back to something. Tell us how you decided Lauren Mancone is shooting people."

"I remember."

"What do you remember?"

"Kel walks Booger."

Mojtabai sits up, recognizing Al has identified a pattern of activity that may be related to the murders.

"That is good information. May I call you Al?"

"Al."

"Al, what do you think is important about when Kel walks his dog, Booger?"

"Not walks."

"Please explain."

Carin slides her hand along the table with a gesture of a raised index finger, asking Mojtabai to wait. The detective knows Al is frightened.

"Al, I know you are nervous. When you get nervous, you stop using your words. We need you to use your words so we can understand what you are telling us."

"They died when Kel didn't walk Booger."

"I think I understand. Did you correlate the days the people were murdered to the days Kel did not walk Booger?"

"Yes. Correlated."

"That is good work. Excellent work. Wait here."

Carin rushes out and quickly returns with a folder. Opening the folder, it has one piece of paper. Carin shows Al the note.

"A little girl walking with her mother gave me this a few days ago. It says: *Find the Booger*. Do you know anything about this note?"

"Laura."

"The woman I saw with the girl, the one on the sidewalk, I thought it might be Laura. Is Laura the girl's mother?"

"Aunt."

"Laura is the girl's aunt."

"Did you give this note to Laura so she could give it to me?"

"Yes."

"Why not give it to me yourself? Al, use your words."

Al looks at Mojtabai and then back to the table. Carin seizes the moment.

"I think I may know why you are being uncommunicative. You want you and me to have credit for the pattern you found. Agent Mojtabai is our new partner and has complete access to information. I need you to use your words and tell us what you think is important about the days Kel walks Booger."

"Nurse-Doctor Louie kills people when Kel is away."

"Away? Business trips? How do you know to call him Kel?"

"Kel told me his name when I petted Booger."

"Do you see Kel and Booger often?"

"Every day. They live near my street."

Mojtabai leans forward.

"I think I understand. Kel walks Booger every day except when he is away on business. Al, partner, this is good information. Louie and Kel are suspects. Partner, you can't mention our work to anyone. Please tell me you understand."

"It is confidential."

Al returns Carin's smile with a rocking nod, allowing Mojtabai to continue.

"With Kelvin traveling at the same time as the murders, we have a solid lead. I think it's time we interview Nurse-Doctor Louie and her husband, Kel."

Carin places her palm on the table, telling Mojtabai to slow down.

"This information is *confidential*. Please tell me you will not speak about this to anyone. Not your parents. Not Laura. No one can know other than Agent Mojtabai and me. Tell me you understand the importance of not telling anyone what we know."

Mojtabai cringes at what he thinks are condescending instructions from the detective. Al doesn't look up with his statement.

"Everything is confidential. Premature release of the

line of inquiry could jeopardize the investigation."

Al has stunned Mojtabai. Carin recognizes Al is quoting a crime drama.

"Yes, Al, that is exactly right. Thank you for bringing it to our attention. Now, I think you should go home. Remember what the chief told you. Be sure to let your mother know you are okay. I will contact you tomorrow or the next day. If you get any new emails, forward them to me right away. Okay?"

"Yes."

Mojtabai runs for a bio break while Carin escorts Al from the building. Also, taking advantage of the pause in the discussion for a bio break gives Carin time to think. Back in the conference room, the detective jumps to the point.

"Well, *Special Agent Mosh*, we have a solid lead."

Mosh gives as good as he gets and copies Al's use of odd phrasing for people's names and titles.

"*Detective Carin*, can we trust your new partner to keep quiet?"

"I think Al takes his work seriously. We need to act quickly to ensure the information doesn't leak. Mosh, we'll ask the chief to call in a favor and expedite the warrant. If you agree, interviewing Louie and Kelvin is priority number one."

"I agree. I'd also like to speak with Laura about Al and the note."

"You can't."

"I can't? I can speak to anyone I think might have relevant information."

"Sorry. Laura is nonverbal."

"How does she communicate?"

"A combination of signing and texts."

"Texts? We can do the same. Where is Laura?"

"Mosh, I'm not sure. I don't know Laura's last name. We can start at the facility."

"You are referring to the ASD training center. The one in your location log?"

"Yes."

"Won't it be tough to communicate with someone who is nonverbal? Should we call in a specialist?"

"There's an app for everything. I learned how to use a speech recognition app to accelerate sending texts. Laura hears perfectly well. She doesn't speak."

"I see. That's something. I know technology is opening doors for people with special needs. Now, I will see it in person."

"Technology has opened a lot of doors and is a game changer for a lot of people. Let's go."

Carin's mind fills with a memory of her mother teaching her to read. The pain of her mother's death begins to rise. Before it can create the panic she knows is lurking, she returns to her counseling sessions and something one of the other group liked to repeat. *"There is no app for fixing pain. The tools we need to cope with mental agony are in our heads."*

In the conference room of the ASD facility, Carin confirmed that her and Laura's phones can send and receive texts. Placing her phone between herself and Mojtabai, Carin looks across the table at Al's friend Tawni Laura-Mara Pritchett.

"Hello Laura, thank you for agreeing to chat with us. I am Detective Trimble, and this is Special Agent Mojtabai. We want to ask you a few questions. If that is okay."

Trimble and Mojtabai do not have to wait long for Laura to type her response — her fingers fly across the tiny keyboard on her phone.

Laura-Mara Pritchett
Hello. You are here to talk about Al.

"Yes. Has Al spoken to you about what he is working on?"

Laura-Mara Pritchett
Sort of.

"When did he ask you to give me the note?"
Laura's keying is lightning-fast. Still, patience is needed. Carin and Mojtabai force pleasant faces.

Laura-Mara Pritchett
Al was here when we saw you at the café.
Visiting Gracy and me.
Laura-Mara Pritchett
He wrote a note to give to you.

"Is Gracy your niece?"

Laura-Mara Pritchett
Yes. Grace. We call her Gracy.

"Did you wonder about the note? What did it mean?"

Laura-Mara Pritchett
I thought Al was playing one of his jokes.

"Is Al a funny guy?"

Laura-Mara Pritchett
Al likes to laugh.

Shocked at learning about a side of Al she has not seen, Carin defers to Mojtabai, sliding her phone slightly toward the special agent. "Miss Pritchett, how long have you known Al?"

Laura-Mara Pritchett
All my life.

"Did you meet Al here, at the facility?"

Laura-Mara Pritchett
At the pool.

"Pool?"

Laura-Mara Pritchett
Recreation center. I learned to walk in the
water.

"About the note. Did Al say anything about its meaning or why he demanded you give it to Detective Trimble?"

Laura-Mara Pritchett
No demand. He asked.
I don't know what it means.

"You thought the note was Al playing a joke?"

Laura-Mara Pritchett
Yes.

"I think we have enough. Thank you, Miss Pritchett, for your time."

Laura-Mara Pritchett
Is Al in trouble? Did Al kill those people?

Waving a frantic no, Carin pulls her phone close and remembers Mosh needs to see the screen.

"No, no, no. Nothing like that. We are trying to figure out how all the pieces fit together. The note was Al being funny."

Laura-Mara Pritchett
Al is a good man.

"Al is a good man. Thank you, Laura."

* * *
** ** **

"I can see you like it. I told you, this café has good scones and coffee. What do you think about the chat with Laura?"

Mosh swallows the oversized bite of scone to answer Carin's inquiry.

"Good scone. I think you should tell me what *you* think. It's your case. You have the history."

"This is not how I expected the investigation to proceed."

"You expected me to come in and kick you to the curb."

"Well. Yes."

"I don't work that way. Other special agents might. Not me. Now, what do you think about Laura?"

"I think she is a non-starter. Al saw an opportunity and used it to get the dog's name on my radar."

"Exactly my thought. By the way, did you see the warrants came through? Your chief has pull."

"It's a small community. How do you want to proceed?"

"Do you have a couple of troopers you trust?"

"Patrol officers? Sure."

"A male and a female?"

Grasping the implications, Carin unwrinkled her forehead at Mosh's odd request.

"One male, one female. Yes."

"Let's chat with the chief — he needs to approve a few hours of overtime."

"Overtime? I don't follow."

"Overtime for the troopers you are going to call and ask to help us. We are going to interview the Mancones after work hours. I'll interview Kelvin with the male trooper. At the same time, you interview Lauren with the female. Scripted, video, audio, by the book."

"When? How?"

"The how is easy. We will send the troopers to do the pick-up in an unmarked car and plain clothes. Say, 7:00, after dinner. We want to keep a low profile until we know Lauren or Kel is our killer. The when depends. We will send the troopers on the pickup run as soon as Chief Johnston approves the overtime."

"Mosh, Al thinks the killer is a woman. I tend to agree. The indicators point to a female, in a nurse's uniform, as the person doing the shooting."

"Which is why you are going to talk to Lauren. Statistically, it is unlikely a woman has killed this many people."

"Let me call the chief."

Mojtabai sips coffee and noshes scone while listening to Carin's side of her chat with the chief.

"Yes, Mosh is here with me. We're good. Mosh and I want to interview the Mancones.

"Yes.

"Here's the catch. We want the Mancones picked up after hours.

"Yes, low-profile.

"I want to send Emily Hansen and Quentin Meyer in

plain clothes, in an unmarked, to pick up the Mancones.

"Agreed.

"Emily will sit in with me and Lauren. Quentin will sit in with Mosh and Kelvin.

"By the book.

"Thanks, Chief."

Sliding her phone into her front pants pocket and downing the last drops of coffee, Carin is apprehensive about her update for the special agent.

"We have the approval."

Chapter Fourteen

In Interrogation Room A, Carin sits beside Emily Hansen and across from Lauren Mancone.

"Mrs. Mancone, thank you for agreeing to speak with us. You are not under arrest and are free to leave at any time. You've met Deputy Hansen. I am Detective Trimble. Everything is being recorded."

Looking to her left, the video image displays the date and time.

"The date and time are confirmed correct. I'd like to ask you a few questions about recent deaths."

"Do I need a lawyer?"

"That is up to you. Do you want to have a lawyer present?"

Before Lauren Mancone can answer, the door opens. Agent Mojtabai steps in, closes the door and stands behind Carin and Deputy Hansen with his back to the wall. Suspecting Kelvin Mancone has demanded an attorney, Carin returns to questioning Lauren.

"Joining us is Special Agent Mojtabai. Lauren, tell me about the days Kelvin travels. We presume business trips are why he has made ten visits to Denver and Dallas in the last eighteen months?"

Sitting tall, stiffening her back, Lauren Mancone has ice in her voice in response to the detective's question.

"Tell you about the days? Are you asking me what he does when he travels for work? I don't know what he does on his trips. As far as I know, he manages the software development team and keeps the work aligned with the project goals. What are you saying? You are making me uncomfortable with your insinuations and accusations."

"It is not our intent to make you uncomfortable. My apologies. Lauren, what do you do when Kelvin is away on business?"

"What do I do? I do what everyone does. Take care of the dog. Go to work. Clean the house. What is this about?"

"Does anyone visit you when Kelvin is out of town on business?"

"Why would anyone visit me? I don't like your implication. I think I want a lawyer."

"That is your right. One more question. What do you know about the cancer patients being shot?"

"Nothing. Do you think I killed those people?"

"No, we are just trying to tie up loose ends."

"You think I am a loose end? I want a lawyer. Right now."

* * *
** ** **

With a look of curiosity on Quentin's face, Emily Meyer returned from the washroom to join the trio of Carin, Mojtabai, and Quentin in the hallway. Carin wants feedback before ordering the deputies to take the Mancones home and end the long day.

"Meyer, what do you think?"

"She's not the killer. She thinks she knows who is doing the killing."

"That's interesting. What gives you the belief Mrs. Mancone knows who is doing the killing?"

"I dunno. A hunch. I felt Mrs. Mancone was worried about being blamed. I think she knows and could probably give up the person doing the shooting."

"Hansen?"

"Nothing important to add. Mr. Mancone refused to speak without an attorney. One thing to note about what happened — neither spoke after we picked them up."

"Both were silent all the way to the office?"

"Yes."

"Thank you both. Agent Mojtabai?"

"Nothing more. Thank you. Troopers, collect the Mancones, take them home, listen for anything."

"Will do."

"Will do."

In the chief's conference room, which has turned into the investigation's command post, Carin waits for Mojtabai to speak.

"Kelvin has a history he doesn't want Lauren to know about. Maybe the business trips are hiding an alternate life."

"We have his file. What history? What life? Nothing points to Kelvin Mancone."

Mosh recites data from memory, confirming to Carin he has read all the materials she has collected.

"Something was redacted from his file. He probably had a drug bust when he was a teenager. That wouldn't be in his file. Kelvin Mancone has a minor offense, probably pot-related. He's not our killer. With his credit cards and phone records, we can easily prove that Kel was out of town when most murders occurred."

Carin's head bobs in agreement with her comments.

"That leaves us with Lauren. Did something seem odd to you about her attitude? We can subpoena Lauren's cell phone records. I'll bet a scone her phone was at home or work during the murders."

Mosh is unmoved by Carin's assertion about Lauren Mancone.

"Agreed, she seemed too calm for someone who thinks we are investigating her as a serial killer. Hunches and observations are not proof. We need more."

An hour of case review and speculative analysis ends with Mojtabai kindly pulling rank.

"Carin, go home. We start again tomorrow morning."

The door opens, and Duty Sergeant Jan Kolston steps in and speaks to Carin without introduction.

"Detective, your partner was attacked. He was admitted to Hemingway County Medical Center."

Carin scrunches her forehead at the day-shift duty sergeant being on watch at this late hour.

"Jan, why are you here at this hour?"

"Sergeant Monk called in sick. I'm covering her shift."

"My partner was attacked? Do you mean Al Demchuk?"

"That's the guy."

"How do you know?

"The ER called."

"The ER called, asking for me?"

"Detective, you know what I know."

The duty sergeant strides away, ending the discussion.

*** *** ***

Carin arrives at the emergency room to find Al has been moved to a patient room. Like many small community hospitals, Hemingway County Medical Center is brimming with patients while struggling financially. Staff shortages and rising costs are the headlines documenting the slow demise of another rural hospital.

Arriving at the correct room, Carin finds John and Deena Demchuk on the other side of the bed. She ignores Deena's steely-eyed daggers aimed her way. Carin moves to the end of Al's bed, accepting his weak smile with a similar smile. Deena speaks and confirms Momma Bear is unhappy that the detective came to see her son.

"You did this."

"Mrs. Demchuk, I am sorry, I had nothing to do with Al getting hurt. How did it happen? Why was I called?"

"I told them to call you."

"Thank you, Mr. Demchuk. Al, What happened?"

Deena's protective nature is overflowing. She interrupts before her son can respond.

"I have told Al to stay away from the crime scenes. You did this."

"Mom, it's okay. Detective Carin is my friend."

"Mrs. Demchuk, I've also warned your son to stay away from the investigation. Al, can you tell me what happened when you were hurt?"

John pulls his wife into the hall for a break and to get her to calm down.

"Partner, what happened?"

"I was hit on the head. Like you."

"Where?"

"Right here, by my ear."

"Sorry. Where were you when you were hit on the head?"

"Walking."

"Walking where?"

Al looks away at the sharp question. Carin realizes her mistake, breathes, calms herself, and forces a soothing tone into her question.

"Where were you when you were hit on the head?"

"Walk-about. I like walk-about. I was thinking about the cases. I got a new email."

"Do you think the person who hit you is the person who hit me in Tercia LeClare's room?"

"Maybe."

Moving from the end of the bed to the side vacated by Mrs. Demchuk, Carin is closer to her partner, making it easier for Al to see her face. Something is odd about Al, and Carin cannot decide what is wrong with her partner.

"A new email? Do you know who is going to be next?"

"No."

"Are you sure?"

"Yes."

"Yes, you know, or yes, you are sure you do not know?"

"I don't know."

"What do you need to figure out who is next?"

"I can't figure it out. Nurse-Doctor Louie is the killer."

Al's tone and facial stiffness are odd and unusual. Carin is sure something is wrong with the man in the bed.

"No, Al, we know that's not true."

A bluebird lighting on the windowsill distracts Al. There is just enough light from the room to highlight the iridescent nature of the bird's wings.

"Al? Stay with me. What is next in your investigation? What is in the new email?"

"Wait. Birds are flying at night because of the lights."

"Wait for what? Help me understand."

"I don't know who is next."

"Why do you want me to wait?"

Carin realizes her pleading is stressing Al. Almost in a whisper, she successfully catches his desire to help.

"I don't understand."

"Someone else will die."

"Who?"

"I am tired. It is time to sleep."

Carin finds the Demchuks in the waiting room. A deputy patrol officer stands to the side, waiting to take a statement. The patrol officer defers to the detective.

"Can you tell me what happened?"

John Demchuk squeezes his wife's arm. Deena understands her husband's message and remains silent while John reports the incident to the detective.

"Deena had just come in from the grocery store when

Al stumbled into the kitchen. He was bleeding from the cut over his ear. I called 911, and they told me to take Al to the ER. Here we are."

"Did Al say anything about where he was or what he saw?"

"Detective, when Al is hurt, he clams up. Always has. Once, he cut his hand with a box cutter and needed a few stitches. He didn't speak for a week. Give him a few days, and he'll start talking."

"This deputy will take your statements. Thank you."

Carin ignores Deena's wicked scowl and walks away after a slight nod for the pleasant John Demchuk.

Watching the frozen breakfast sandwich thaw under the bombardment of invisible energy, Carin has a minor epiphany. Pulling the mostly thawed sausage biscuit from the machine, the detective rushes to the office.

Mojtabai is waiting for Carin to arrive in their investigation's workroom. Mosh looks up from his PC as Carin sits and opens her PC. Not waiting for Carin to settle in, Mosh sees the new detective's agitation and asks with a lilt.

"What happened?"

"Al was out for a walk when someone hit him from

behind on the side of the head. They kept him overnight for observation. He will be okay."

"I know. Here is the report from the patrol officer."

Mosh slides the folder toward Carin. She pushes it aside and reaches for the breakfast she brought while eyeing the bagels at the end of the table.

"Let me read it. Did you buy bagels?"

"Yes."

Carin tosses her half-thawed, half-eaten sausage sandwich in the trash. She grabs a bagel with maple-walnut spread and a thick, dark coffee, then sits to read the report.

"Oh."

"What?"

Carin does not respond. She flips back and begins rereading the incident report.

"Detective Trimble?"

"Sorry, Mosh. According to Deena Demchuk, Al was two houses down from the Mancone residence when he was struck. The Mancones live two blocks over and one north of the Demchuks."

Jumping directly to the end, Mojtabai asks.

"Does the timing work?"

"I think so. The deputies would have dropped off the Mancones a few minutes before the attack on Al."

Mashing the speaker button on the conference room phone, Carin presses the extension for the duty sergeant.

"*Sergeant Kolston.*"

"Jan? Are you still here?"

"*I am back.*"

"This is Detective Trimble."

"I know your voice — what's up?

Surprised at Jan Kolston's flippant tone, Carin chalks it up to three shifts in two days.

"I need Deputies Hansen and Meyer on a conference call ASAP."

"On it."

Carin ends the call, looks up, swallows her bagel, sips, bites again, and speaks through the glob of dough and maple-walnut spread.

"I think the Mancones need a lawyer."

"Hold on. You are making leaps and connections without proof."

Carin presses the speaker button when the phone chimes.

"I have Meyer and Hansen."

"Hello."

"Hello."

"Thank you, Sergeant Kolston. Please stay on the line. I have Special Agent Mojtabai with me. Hansen, tell me what happened when you took the Mancones home."

"Nothing happened."

"Nothing?"

"Nope. They didn't speak. Got out of the car and didn't look back."

"Did they enter the house?"

"Yes. Then we drove away."

"Meyer."

"I concur with Hansen."

"Sergeant, I'm going to screw with the duty rosters. I want Hansen and Meyer to canvas Fifth Street — every house, one block north and one south of the Mancone residence. Start in front of the house where Al Demchuk was assaulted. Look for clues, knock on doors. Sergeant, make sure the incident report is available on the computer. Of course, Deputies, please look for anyone who saw or heard anything. Also, look for security and doorbell cameras. See if anyone has Al Demchuk walking on video. Agent Mojtabai?"

"Of course, this is confidential. Otherwise, nothing to add."

"Sergeant?"

"I'm on it. Hansen, Meyer, civvies, and an unmarked. I'll see you in thirty minutes."

Carin, pressing the red button and terminating the call, begins hours of discussion and investigation review that turns up no new ideas or leads. When the phone rings, interrupting the monotony of analysis, Carin presses the green button.

"Sergeant Kolston here. Meyer and Hansen finished the canvas and will arrive in five."

"Thank you, Sergeant."

Rising for a bio break, Mojtabai gives his culture's native side-to-side head nod and says what Carin is thinking.

"Maybe we'll get lucky."

Emily Hansen has a serious look on her face. Carin notices Quentin Meyer's face is softer. *"He is pleased with something they found canvasing the neighborhood."*

With seniority over Meyer, Hansen waves, giving the junior officer permission to report.

"We have video from a doorbell camera. I gave it to Sergeant Kolston to give to forensics. They will check for viruses, then load the video to the case file."

Meyer stops speaking, confusing Carin and Mojtabai. Hansen breaks the tension with her pleasing voice.

"In the video, an unknown person is seen rushing up behind the victim. In the shadows, the attacker appears to wear black sneakers and nurse's scrubs, with a black hoodie pulled high and cinched tight. The attacker strikes the victim with an unknown device. Hopefully, forensics can pull more information from the video."

Carin and Mojtabai eye each other, their sad realization filling the room. Mosh uses his training to control his voice.

"Good work, deputies. Of course, this is confidential. Thank you."

Meyer and Hansen rise to leave when Emily speaks.

"Detective Trimble, may I speak with you privately?"

After receiving an approving chin thrust from Mojtabai, Carin waits for Meyer and the investigation's FBI lead to close the door on their way out of the conference room.

"Detective Trimble."

"Carin."

"Carin, the person in the video is not Lauren Mancone."

"From what you and Meyer reported, there is no way to identify the attacker. How can you exclude Lauren Mancone?"

When Hansen hesitates, Carin recognizes the deputy wants to admit something.

"Deputy Hansen, this is between you and me."

"Call me Emily."

"Emily, whatever it is, it will stay between you and me."

After breathing deeply, sucking in strength, Deputy Hansen admits something for the first time.

"The attacker is not tall enough to be Lauren Mancone. Also."

Emily's strength has faded quickly, and she goes quiet with glazed-over eyes. Carin is kind.

"That's good information. Forensics can use photographic analysis to determine a person's height. Emily, I can see you have something else. What else do you want to say?"

"The attacker's behind was too wide."

Patrol officer Hansen has admitted to admiring Lauren Mancone's body. Waiting until the deputy returns her look, Carin soothes Emily's fear.

"Emily, that is a good observation. I will ask forensics for a detailed photogrammetry analysis. All they need is more than one image to create the 3D representation. Emily?"

"Yes, Carin?"

"Your secret is safe with me."

"Thank you."

"Send in Agent Mojtabai — if he is not waiting with his ear to the door."

The mental image of an FBI special agent with his ear to a door causes Emily to grin. Mojtabai is, of course, waiting in the hallway for the door to open.

"Well? Carin, what do you have?"

"Agent Mojtabai, Lauren Mancone is not the attacker. She could be the killer. If she is, she didn't hit Al in the head."

"How can you know?"

"I just know, and photogrammetry will prove the person in the crappy video is not Lauren Mancone."

Chapter Fifteen

"Al, you have to eat."

"Deena, Al will eat if he is hungry."

"Shut up, John. Al, you have to eat."

John knows his wife is reverting to the person everyone warned him about. Long past worrying about what she might do, John Demchuk stares down his wife and tells her again that he is tired of her threats and will not be bullied.

"No, Deena. Al is a grown man. He can choose to eat or not."

Weeks of Al being in a funk are stressful for the small family. Deena takes it in stride — nothing is wrong with her precious boy. John knows his son's not eating is a sign of depression. He waits for Deena to collect Al's uneaten porridge before continuing to try to help his troubled son.

"Al, do you want to tell me what is bugging you?"

"No."

"Is it about the investigation?"

Al refuses to respond.

"What is going on with the investigation? You knew the special agent would take over the case. You knew that you and Detective Trimble would support the federal investigator. I thought you liked Agent Mojtabai. Did something happen?"

"It is a cold case."

"Do you mean they have stopped actively investigating the murders?"

"Yes."

"Does that mean the case won't be solved?"

"Maybe."

"What are you going to do today? With the investigation moving to cold status, you should find a way to fill your time. Son, there are many part-time job openings for the city and county on their websites."

"I have a job."

"I am aware you consider the investigations your job. Maybe a job that pays is an option. If you earned money, you could take more trips."

"I am a detective."

"Yes, son, you are a detective. We have talked about reality and television. Not all television programs are accurate. You know that not all cases are solved, especially murders committed by someone who is skilled and intelligent. It may take years, if ever, to confirm the killer's identity.

"Dad, I'm an investigator. I solve mysteries."

"Son, let me help you."

"You can't help. I know who killed the terminated people."

"*Knowing* and *proving* are two different things. I am aware that Detective Trimble and Agent Mojtabai have told you that knowing is not proof. Al, please. Maybe it's time to find a new job."

"I don't want a new job."

Deena stops watching her husband try to reason with her stubborn son. Rolling her eyes and turning away is Al's clue. John watches his son return to his room at the end of the backyard, under the trees and down the slope.

Watching the broken microwave count down another preservative-laden breakfast, Carin decides to buy a new microwave and gain a new perspective. Frustrated and annoyed with life, she is willing to try anything to break the cloud shrouding her mind. Maybe shopping for a new microwave will yank her mindset from the negative spiral of failure, and today is a sparring day at the dojo. Sparring is always good for a mental reset.

* * *

"Hajimari!"

Carin always smiles when she is on the sparring mat, and the Sensei barking the instruction to begin widens her grin. The tatami fibers feel good on her bare feet. In this dojo, light blows to the body are permitted. Head strikes are supposed to be pulled. Stopping short of hitting your opponent's face with your fist, elbow, foot, or shin shows discipline and respect.

Knocking down a less experienced opponent is uncommon. Carin's sparring partner has an eye blackening before he hits the mat. Striking an opponent in the head once is not accepted. Hitting someone in the face, three sparring sessions in a row, shows a lack of discipline and lousy character.

"*Yame!*" Stop!

"Sensei, forgive me. I'm distracted."

"You may take a break. Go home and think about our teachings. *Take a break.* In a week, we will discuss when you are ready to return to the dojo."

A respected detective hurting yet another inexperienced student is terrible for business. Still, Carin knows her Sensei's ban is his way of protecting her from herself.

* * *

Driving to the office two months after the last murder, Carin mentally runs down the status of the stalled investigation. Her mind is all over the details. She returns every few minutes to wonder if Mojtabai will formally declare it a cold case and move on to his next assignment. Her thoughts are flying, including memories from her childhood and her mother. The randomness of her thoughts grate on her meticulous nature.

"*The coroner, Marc, thinks thirteen bodies are connected and possible murders. We know the last three are murders. We can't link the killings to each other or a specific person. Maybe the victims were dead when their hearts exploded. Al knows too much. He cannot, or will not, share the background. Al is hiding something — he is not the killer. Could it be Al?*

"*No DNA is odd. There is always some touch DNA. How can there be no DNA? Someone is too intelligent. Like 'doctor of oncology' smart. Greene knows her work is going sideways.*

That is a supposition and is probably accurate. She made promises of no pain that were untrue. Could Greene be the killer out of the deep-seated desire for patient sympathy and maybe empathy?

"Is Louie Mancone protecting her boss? Is Kel Mancone helping his wife by offing the patients who prove Greene's trial is a failure?

"Every thread unravels into a long line of nothing. There are no genuine leads or confirmed suspects. There are people of interest, and nothing is pointing to one person. Maybe it is more than one person?

"None of it matters. Mojtabai will call it cold, the chief will support the Feds, and I will be known as the person who failed to solve her first big case."

* * *
** ** **

After being kicked out of the chief's conference room, Carin squatted in IR-B. At the table in the small conference room, diving back into the case data, eyeing her map and the classic red yarn connecting the murder locations, Carin is resigned to not solving the Nursing Home Murders.

Correctly adjusting the location pins and moving a red line on the map, a defeated Carin slumps into a chair. Looking up, she realizes the red lines create a distorted star with the center encircling the town of Marble Grove. The red star is a symbol that surrounds her failure as a detective. The bird chirping from her phone snaps her mind into the present. Taking her thoughts off the data does not cover the stench of failure.

"Detective Trimble."

"It's Mosh. I received the second forensic analysis from our lab in Virginia. I'm forwarding the reports now. Heads up, same as before, there is no unaccounted-for DNA."

"That is not good news."

"No, it is not. Also, the emails Al forwarded to you are a non-starter. The team thinks the emails are being manufactured using an obfuscator site."

"If the sender uses an obfuscator email site, they're intelligent enough to hide their tracks."

"We all know serial killers are notorious for being highly intelligent."

"Any more bad news? Mosh, we got nothing."

"This might be something good. Our labs will create something called a speculative report when they cannot definitely determine the root cause. The speculative report for this case suggests looking for a homemade weapon. The report indicates someone is using a handmade tool to fire the bullet and suppress the sound."

"If the killer can make a gun, they can make the bullet extraction tool."

"Agreed."

"When will you return to Marble Grove?"

"Not for a couple of weeks unless there is another murder."

"Is this case confirmed cold?"

"Probably. Not for another couple of months."

"That's just great. *Crime Case Files* will want to interview me about another unsolved series of murders for their true crime drama. My face will be streaming in living rooms across the country."

"Everyone deserves their fifteen minutes."

"I don't want fifteen minutes of fame for being unable to solve my first big case. Thanks for the update."

"Carin, keep your head up. Something will break our way."

"Thanks, Mosh."

*** *** ***

Back from her mother's funeral service and a week of farm work to help her father adjust, Carin is easing into her duties and the failed case of the Nursing Home Murders. After getting the chief's okay for an afternoon off, Carin heads to the big box hardware store to buy the microwave, which she hopes will change her attitude. She'll drive the forty minutes because the retailer of everything construction and home decor gives veterans a discount.

Of course, home appliances are in the furthest corner from the entrance of the concrete building. Walking along, Carin stops at a sales video looping on an endcap. Surrounded by construction power tools that are securely wired to the endcap metal frame, the video describes the interchangeability of the manufacturer's battery-powered devices. Of course, Carin could save $400 if she buys the power tools in a bundle. Batteries are extra.

One of the tools being demonstrated in the sales video catches Carin's attention. The Framer's Nail Gun fires the nails with low-powered twenty-two caliber shells. Reading every word on the nail gun's packaging and searching her phone for videos describing how to use a nail gun, Carin has convinced herself she has an answer.

After dashing to the appliance section, forgetting the research she did to select a device, she buys the first microwave she sees with a familiar brand name. Carin rushes back to the office. Ensuring the conference doors are closed, Carin calls Special Agent Mojtabai.

"Mosh?"

"*Carin?*"

"I think I know how they were killed."

"*I'm listening.*"

"Do you know how they kill cattle at the processing plants?"

"*Not a clue. I don't eat beef.*"

"Have you read *No Country for Old Men* by Cormac McCarthy?"

"*No.*"

"Cattle are lined up in a chute, and a stainless-steel rod, a bolt, is fired into the brain. In the story, the killer uses a bolt gun."

"*I probably didn't need to know that piece of data. What else? Where are you going with this information?*"

"What if the cancer victims weren't shot? Well, what if they were shot and not with a pistol?"

"*That's thin, give me more.*"

"A nail gun is also called a nailer. It is a specialized hammer used to drive nails into wood. There are a few types of nail guns: compressed air, electric, gas like butane or propane, and ours. Our killer uses a nail gun that requires a low-power twenty-two blank cartridge, or compressed air, to operate. We have no powder residue. I'm going with compressed air as the weapon."

"*That's good. How do you prove it?*"

"All nail guns have a safety interlock."

"*And?*"

"And, the safety is released by pressing the small feet, parallel little bars, against the surface being nailed. Marc pointed out parallel lines on the victims."

"*What is up with your people in forensics? Does that new coroner have the tools he needs?*"

"Are you asking if forensics and Marc missed the connection? Mosh, it's not obvious. The marks are small, and not all the victims have dents near the chest wound."

"*You are making excuses for their work.*"

"No. Maybe."

Sighing, the detective continues, trying not to sound whiny.

"Mosh, we don't have easy access to a federally funded lab in the woods of Virginia."

"*Fair — people work with what they have. Good work. I'll be there tomorrow. Get a warrant for sales records in a hundred-mile radius. We want to know who has bought a nail gun in the past year.*"

"Mosh, the murders predate a year. Sales receipts at some of the smaller places will be nonexistent. What if the person paid cash?"

"*Carin, you have to start somewhere. You run down the*

receipts. *Not a deputy, you."*

"That is a lot of ground to cover."

"It is, and do you know why it has to be you?"

Carin leans back, breathes long and hard, accepting the special agent's kind nudge of instruction, and then gives the answer she knows is correct.

"Because someone will remember something, and I can connect the dots."

"Bingo. See you in a couple of days."

Catching her breath and clearing her thoughts, Carin decides to move quickly. Choosing to begin with the chief, poking her head into his office, Carin doesn't wait for her boss to look up.

"Chief, do you have a second?"

"Make it quick."

"I need an open warrant for the sales records for a tool."

Leaning back, the chief's interest is piqued. Repeating what she told Mojtabai, the chief is making the call for the warrant before Carin can turn to leave his office.

"Hold, please."

The chief mutes his phone and looks up to Carin.

"Detective?"

"Chief?"

"Good work. By the book. I know you are amped up. You can't make a mistake now."

"Understood."

After an internet search for hardware retailers of nail guns, and plotting the store locations on her map, Carin is still waiting for the warrant. After checking her map a third time and confirming a search pattern, she decides to go to the café and wait for the records warrant.

Five stores and nearly two hundred miles later, Carin realizes the small hardware stores are unlikely to have sold high-end construction power tools. Big box retailers are sucking the life out of small businesses. Carin refocuses and ignores the memory of buying a microwave from a big box store. Frustrated at the lack of detail in the sales information, Carin sits in her car and thinks.

"Detective 101: Keep it simple."

There is no point in visiting smaller stores. Three big box stores deep in the revised search pattern, the detective learns nail guns are not a high-sales volume item. The store managers, who all have current computer systems, give Carin a list of nail gun sales for the prior 18 to 24 months. After driving across three counties, Carin arrives at where she should have begun — the store that gave her a clue about the murders.

"Hello, is there a manager I can speak to?"

The customer service person with rainbow hair, too many facial piercings, and tattoos on her fingers points to the office behind the counter. Stepping around and looking into the office, the manager has video monitors along the back wall. Spinning his chair forward, he looks up to speak.

"I'm the manager."

"I'm Detective Trimble. I'd like to know if you've sold a

nail gun recently?"

"Not recently."

"Are you sure?"

"I review high-dollar sales every day. No nail guns in a few weeks."

Ignoring the manager's curt tone, Carin persists.

"Can you search your records?"

"Do you have a warrant?"

"Here. I have a question — if I may. None of the managers I have spoken with had to ask permission to provide the information. When I showed the warrant, the information was made available to me. Is that normal?"

Wearing a blue vest, the manager, with a thin, scattered beard and tattoos on his hands and neck, puts the warrant aside without glancing at the paperwork. He eyes Carin while touch-typing on the computer. Carin wonders if the woman at the customer service desk and the manager producing her report are a couple. The manager decides to look at his computer and respond in a flat tone.

"We have training, policies, and procedures for how to respond to police requests. If there is a warrant, we are to comply and then report the incident to corporate."

"Incident?"

"Is interaction a better word?"

Noting the manager is intelligent and articulate eases her tension when he reaches under the side desk. Rising, he staples and then hands Carin two sales pages. Quickly glancing at the pages gives the detective an idea.

"This is every nail gun this location has ever sold.

Thank you. Those video monitors, do you retain the recordings?"

"Yep."

"Yep?"

"It means, yes, we retain the recordings."

Carin refuses to be frustrated with the manager's snarky answers.

"I meant, for how long do you retain the recordings?"

"That's not what you asked. Our policy and instructions are not to answer questions that are legal in nature. Otherwise, we are to respond with as few words as possible."

Carin is a little shocked at the response. She understands when the tattooed finger points to the camera, recording their interaction.

"I will try to be more exacting. Mr...."

"Clarendon."

Glancing again at the sales list, Carin checks the dates of the sales transactions.

"Mr. Clarendon, the last four sales of a nail gun go back thirteen months. Do you have the recording of the sales transactions?"

"Yes."

Sensing an idea is about to emerge, Carin steadies her breathing and presses the manager for information.

"I'll play twenty questions. Can you access the sales recordings from here?"

"Yes."

"The warrant, the one you didn't read, says *all materials*

available to be reproduced, stored in a retrieval system, or transmitted in any form, by any means, related to the investigation documented herein. Will you copy the video of the specific transactions to a flash drive?"

"Yes."

When Clarendon doesn't move, Carin understands the communication gap with ironic frustration.

"I'll buy the damned flash drive."

Clarendon dials the customer service counter.

"Hon, bring me a one-gigabyte flash drive from aisle nineteen. Call Kyle on the radio to meet you there. You'll need his key to open the case. Detective Trimble will give you a credit card."

Carin hears Hon through the door talking into her walkie-talkie.

"Kyle?"

"What's up?"

"Can you bring me a one-gig flash drive?"

"Yep."

Waiting for the flash drive to arrive and watching the customer traffic through the store on the security monitors, Carin's theory begins to become tangible.

Before Clarendon copies the videos, the epiphany lights up Carin's mind. Down to her core, the new detective knows who the killer is and possibly why they are killing people. Carin understands, however, that intuition won't stand up in a courtroom.

Chapter Sixteen

"Carin, what do you have?"

"Good morning to you, too. Mosh, I have a lot of new data. Let's jump to the end. You brought coffee and scones. Lemon-raspberry, nice touch."

"I learn."

Mojtabai pushes the conference room door closed, stuffs a large chunk of scone into his mouth, sits, and waits for Carin to prepare her presentation.

"I have the videos for the last four sales of a nail gun. Three are known local contractors."

"The fourth?"

Carin responds to the question by starting the video. Mojtabai leans in, swallows, and then asks.

"Is that who I think it is?"

"Yes, it is hard to miss that hair. Who is that in the background? Is he waiting? Does he look nervous to you?"

"The video is enough. We have probable cause. What do you want to do next?"

"Mosh, you're the lead."

"Carin, you found it. You work it. I won't let you stub your toe. What next?"

"That's a little condescending."

"Yeah? So what? Do you want to be on point or not?"

Carin recognizes that Mojtabai is deliberately pushing her buttons.

"I'm tougher than you think. What is your point?"

"Tough? We'll see. I am sorry I got pulled away and

wasn't here when you returned from Texas. I don't think I offered condolences on the loss of your mother. My bad. How are you doing with the loss?"

"I'm good. Like everyone who has lost someone, I'll miss Mom at family functions. Dad is a little better every day, and he stays busy with the farm. Some days are worse than others. Every day is a little better than yesterday, Otherwise, I press on. What else is there?"

"Very Marine of you."

"*Semper Fi.*"

"What are you going to do?"

"I'll take Meyer and Hansen with me. Body cameras will be running the whole time. We'll pull her in for questioning and see what she has to say. We'll ask about the man who is following her around."

"What about the press?"

Confused, Carin looks beyond Mosh, then returns before she asks.

"What *about* the press?"

"If it turns out to be nothing, Carin, you will be crucified in the media. The high-profile arrest of a prominent citizen was unnecessary and all that. What else do you have?"

Carin leans back, looks from Mojtabai to the frozen video image, and then back to the investigative lead. The new detective understands this is a learning opportunity. A sly grin creeps across Carin's face. Always smiling, Mojtabai waits. Carin obliges her new friend.

"I have an idea."

* * *
** ** **

"Mrs. Demchuk, I'd like to speak with Al."

"He doesn't want to speak with you."

"I understand your desire to protect your son. We need his help. Please let Al know I am here to see him. I'll wait."

Deena closes the door without agreeing to notify her son of the visitor. Turning gradually on the porch, Carin admires the fastidiously manicured lawn, the crisp paint lines on the window frames, and the well-trimmed bushes.

"John Demchuk knows there is hell to pay if Deena thinks their life has the wart of a dandelion in the lawn or a dead flower on the hydrangea. Why didn't I notice this is the best-kept house on the block? Focus. Mom used to say I was always somewhere else. What did the counselor say? Get out of your head and into the present."

Recognizing Deena is probably not asking her son to come to the door and wishing she had a warrant, Carin's frustration lands an idea.

Carin Trimble
Al, this is Carin. I have an idea. You can help me. I am at the front door.

Al's response text is quick, yet the brief delay feels like an hour for Carin.

Al Demchuk
*Go around to the back.
I'll open the gate.*

Stepping away from the house, looking side to side, Carin remembers the gate in the fence that opens to the pathway leading to the rear of the property. Of course, Deena is glaring at her from the side window when Al greets Carin at the fence.

"Good morning, Al."

"Partner."

"Good morning, *Partner*."

"Good morning."

As expected, Deena moves from the side window to the kitchen window, which allows her to watch her son and Carin descend the slope through the manicured lawn and flower beds to Al's tiny apartment.

"Let's go into your office."

Carin silently follows Al, then waves politely to Deena before stepping in and closing the door.

"I know that you know who committed the murders. You have known for months, and I should have listened to you more carefully. You tried to tell me. I am sorry that I wasn't listening. Al, Partner, I am listening now. Will you help me with information to confirm and arrest the murderer?"

Al is unusually calm and still. Uncharacteristically, he is looking back at Carin. The detective knows he is becoming comfortable with her and is relaxed when they are alone.

"Will we take walks? I'll get a dog — a basenji. We can take walks. With Laura."

"Yes, partner, we can take walks. I think you won't

want me around while walking with Laura. We will see what it's like with a new dog and a new friend. Yes, I'll walk with you."

"Laura likes you."

"What makes you say that?"

"Laura said you are nice to me."

"Thank you, Al. Will you help me?"

"Yes. What do I do?"

"Come with me to the station. We'll visit with Agent Mojtabai. He and I will make the arrest if we get the correct information."

"I don't want to be there."

"When we make the arrest? That's okay. I'll make sure someone takes you home before the arrest." Carin had not expected Al to be part of the team arresting the murderer.

"I want to name the dog Marti."

Shocked into silence, Carin understands the moment. Her unofficial partner understands she is giving him credit for solving the murders.

"Al, that is a nice name. What made you think of Marti as the name for a dog?"

"That was your name in school."

Carin is stunned.

"How do you know that?"

"It's on-the-line. The schoolbook has your picture."

"My high school yearbook is online? Al, why where you looking for my history?"

"It's on-the-line when you type Carin Marcia Trimble."

"You searched my name, and it linked you to my high

school yearbook. Okay. I think. Let's go."

Al grabs his jacket, confirms his wallet, makes sure the computer and television are off, steps onto the porch, and then waits to close and lock the door behind his partner.

Under Deena's stern glare from the kitchen window, Al and Carin depart. They smartly chose the side gate and the driveway — avoiding going through the house and encountering an angry Mom. Carin's mind is pulling forward the memory of the drama club. Under the picture of the drama club in her senior yearbook, Carin is listed as *Marti Trimble*. One person has called her Marti — Naani Presinda, head of the student drama club. Pushing aside the memory of her mother trying to mend the broken heart of her first love lost, Carin waits for Al to insert the seatbelt buckle before pulling away from the curb.

*** *** ***

"Al, you've met Agent Mojtabai."

"Hello, Al."

"Special Agent Mosh. Can I have a scone?"

"Yes, of course."

Al sits at the end of the table and begins slowly picking apart the day-old lemon-raspberry scone. Carin steps away and returns with the chief. The crushing silence between Al and Mojtabai is broken by the police chief entering his small conference room.

"Hello, Al."

"Uncle Myron."

"You know to call me Uncle Al. It's okay. I know you're upset. We didn't listen closely to you and should have been better at our jobs. Maybe we could have saved one or two of the victims."

"They would die soon."

"Yes, Al, they would have died by now. Please use the correct words. You're a good man."

Carin adds to the chief's praise.

"Laura will be proud of you."

Without a word, Al pulls out his phone and begins texting. The trio thinks Al is texting Laura.

Al Demchuk
Mom, come get me.

Al refuses to look anywhere other than his phone.

Deena Demchuk
I'll be there in five minutes.

Carin recognizes Al is about to become uncommunicative. She desperately wants his cooperation with her arrest plan.

"Al, I know this is hard. We have the proof we need to make the arrest. Please, speak to me. Tell me we can count on you."

Al refuses to look away from the now blank screen on his phone. Under the growing silence, Carin, Mojtabai, and the chief eye each other. Carin motions toward the chief, requesting he try to get Al to engage.

"Al, we'll find you a dog. Carin mentioned you told her you want a Basenji. Is that right? We need your help. From all the good work you did learning about the murderer, anything you may know will help us to confirm who killed those people."

Al responds without looking up.

"Basenji."

"That's a nice dog. Do you think Kel will walk his dog with you and your new dog?"

Al shrugs and does not look up. The chief shuffles before hitting on a lesson he learned from his brother-in-law, John. Changing the subject, intending to return, he persists with Al.

"I think Kel will walk his dog with you. Maybe he will pay you to walk his dog. That's a nice job — dog walker."

Al's tone is flat.

"Kel will move away with Booger."

Carin leans in.

"Maybe. That is a possibility. People move all the time. Al, what we are asking you is important. You know that, right?"

"It is important."

The conference room phone chimes — Carin mashes the green button and then the speaker button.

"Detective Trimble."

"Detective Trimble, Sergeant Kolston. We have Deena Demchuk here demanding to see her son. Also, three other people say they are here to see you."

Wide-eyed, Carin looks around and sees equally wide eyes on Mojtabai. The chief is calm. Looking at his nephew, he gives the orders.

"Sergeant, escort Mrs. Demchuk and the others to my conference room."

"Right away."

Carin is calm when she rises, awaiting the arrival of Mrs. Demchuk. Mojtabai tries to ease Al's mind.

"Al, partner, this is a good thing. Thank you."

Carin and the chief respond simultaneously to the knock on the conference room door.

"Enter." "Enter."

The desk sergeant leads Dr. Greene, Lauren Mancone, Jared McKinnon, and Deena Demchuk into the chief's now-overcrowded conference room. The chief diverts before the women can sit.

"Sergeant Kolston, please take the women to the interview rooms. Dr. Greene and Mrs. Mancone, thank you for coming. Deena, Mister McKinnon, the detectives will be with you shortly."

Sergeant Kolston requests confirmation of the chief's orders.

"Chief?"

"Put Dr. Greene and Mrs. Mancone in IR-A. Mrs. Demchuk in IR-B. Kick out the squatters and put Mister McKinnon in the small conference room."

Carin interrupts. She remembers a conversation with Mosh about Green and Mancone not being on the same page.

"Jan, please put Dr. Greene and Mrs. Mancone in the small conference room and McKinnon in IR-B. Al can wait with his mother in IR-A. Sorry, Al, please remain here. Everyone, the interview rooms are monitored and recorded. Sergeant."

Kolston's forehead wrinkles at the confusing orders.

"On it. Ladies, this way, please."

The door closing is the chief's signal.

"Another minor change. Al, come with me."

"Where are we going, Uncle Myron?"

"We are going to the observation room. Do you want to be a detective and watch the other detectives when they interview the suspects?"

"Yes."

Carin reaches over and dials the number to the small conference room.

"Hello?"

"Who is this?"

"Who are you?"

"This is Detective Carin Trimble. You are to leave this phone open and exit the conference room immediately."

"Sorry. Yes, this is Cadet Micah Thurber. Leave the phone on?"

"Yes. Get out now."

Across the intercom, Mojtabai and Carin hear people shuffling, and then the conference room door opens and closes. Next, the door opens, and Sergeant Kolston is heard.

"Ladies, the detectives will be with you shortly. Do not open the boxes or touch any of the files. The lavatory is just

down the hall to the left. You can use the lav. You may not leave the building without an escort. If you want to leave, come to the front and find me."

The door closing is followed by what Carin and Mojtabai hoped would happen. Both grin when they hear Greene and Mancone start talking.

"Sharon, did you kill those people?"

"You know better than to ask that question. No, I didn't kill anyone. Did you kill those people?"

"No. What do you think is going to happen to us?"

"I don't know. If these police peckers don't let me get back to work, our lawyers will tear them a new one. Louie, do you think Kel had anything to do with all this?"

"No. I mean, I don't think so. According to the news graphic I saw, Kel was in Denver or Dallas when some of the murders occurred. Also, they would have read us our rights if we were under arrest. We are not under arrest. I'll bet Sergeant Kolston won't let us leave without Trimble's okay."

"That's what I thought. When I reported Trimble asking about our patients, the lawyers told me I was too hard on the detective. They told me to ease up. I don't know what it is — Trimble rubs me the wrong way."

"Sharon, we are not under arrest. We can leave."

"Are you sure?"

"Yes. Growing up on the reservation, we quickly learned that the laws are different inside and outside the rez. Out here, they have to read the Miranda Warning to arrest us."

"We'll wait until they come back. Then, if they don't arrest us, we are out of here."

Carin looks to Mojtabai.

"I think we have what we expected from those two. Do we keep listening?"

"Nah, we kick them loose. There's no there, there."

With a massive grin and relief, she presses the red button to end the intercom connection.

"There is no there, there. Mosh, who's next?"

"McKinnon. Let's go."

Chapter Seventeen

Mojtabai checks the video monitor above the recording device on the table, confirms the cameras have the correct angles, and speaks before the door closes on IR-B. While he is taking a seat across the table, Carin and Mojtabai observe Jared McKinnon pouring sweat. The small man's pits have soaked through his suit jacket — his face is dripping onto his pant leg.

"For the record, I am Special Agent Karim Mojtabai. With me is Detective Carin Trimble. The date and time of the video recording are accurate. We are interviewing Jared Carol McKinnon. Mr. McKinnon, do you live at 1787 North Marble Quarry Circle?"

"Yes. What am I doing here? Do I need a lawyer?"

"Do you want an attorney present?"

"Am I under arrest?"

"Carin?"

"Jared Carol McKinnon, you are under arrest for defrauding the city of Marble Grove and the counties of Hemingway, Twekonda, and Juinera. Additionally, you are charged with the willful alteration of a crime scene. Also known as tampering with evidence, you admitted to destroying evidence. However, it is noted your actions were without the intent to interfere with an investigation."

Carin stops, opens her phone, and reads the required legal wording.

"You have the right to remain silent and refuse to answer questions. Do you understand?"

"Yes."

"Anything you choose to say may be used against you in a court of law. Do you understand?"

"Yes."

"You have the right to consult an attorney before speaking to the police and to have an attorney present during questioning, now or in the future. Do you understand?"

"Yes."

Carin catches a whiff of McKinnon's body. Unsure of the smell, the detective assumes it is a mixture of body odor and chemicals mortuaries use to process bodies.

"If you cannot afford an attorney, one will be appointed for you before any questioning if you wish. Do you understand?"

"Yes. I can't afford an attorney. I'll get one if I have to. Do I need an attorney?"

The detective continues as if she did not hear the question.

"If you decide to answer questions now without an attorney present, you will still have the right to stop answering at any time until you talk to an attorney. Do you understand?"

"Yes. I will answer your questions."

"Knowing and understanding your rights as I have explained them to you, are you willing to answer my questions without an attorney present?"

Squirming, wiping his forehead and cheeks with his hand, then smearing the sweat on his faded suit pant leg,

McKinnon answers just above a whisper.

"Yes."

"Thank you. Why are you nervous?"

"I've never been arrested."

"That is understandable. We want to speak about the fraud you have been committing. We also have a few questions — for another investigation."

"What questions." Jared squirms, correctly guessing he is a suspect in the nursing home murders.

"Jared, tell us what your father did before, and what you did, after he passed."

"Dad realized, back in the nineties, that he could be appointed coroner. He had the education and experience. So, he did what was needed."

With a raised eyebrow and a taller spine, Mojtabai is silently telling Carin to press her questions.

"What was needed?"

"Dad paid off the mayor, the city council, and the county board of trustees. Not all of them. He paid enough of them to ensure he had the votes to be appointed coroner. It took every penny he had at the time."

"I understand. Most of those people are no longer alive. Go on." Carin's flat response was direct from her training in interrogation techniques.

"Before the pandemic, Dad would send every second or third body to our business. With my sales skills, it was enough to recoup the investment."

"Investment? You mean bribes."

"Investment. Bribe. The definition depends on where

you stand. We were doing okay. When the pandemic hit, everyone in the industry drank from the fire hose. Cash was pouring in so fast. We couldn't keep up."

"Can we go back to your father for a second? I have a delicate question." Carin interrupting the witness goes directly against the training. Jared squirms in his seat, sighs, anticipates the questions, and blurts before Carin can ask.

"I know what you are going to ask. You have heard the rumors. Everyone in this town has heard the rumors. You are going to ask me if my father was unfaithful to my mother."

"Yes."

"Is the sky blue?"

"Is that a yes?"

"Of course it is."

"Thank you for that information. Back to the mortuary, your father, and the pandemic. Please expand on your statement: *Cash was pouring in so fast.*"

"Bodies are cash in our business. The influx of capital was enough that I upgraded the crematorium and the processing lab."

"Please expand on the upgrade and how you improved the business model."

"Business loans. The federal government promised to make us whole with the relief legislation."

"And?"

"And it wasn't enough money."

Remembering her training, Carin makes a short series

of statements, alluding to facts, then asks an open-ended question that is designed to get the suspect to talk freely.

"I'm not sure I understand the sequence. Let me know if I get anything wrong. Before the pandemic, your father illegally routed deceased people to your funeral home. Ignoring the statutory requirement to rotate city and county funds among the funeral parlors on the list, the McKinnon Funeral Home and Mortuary received more than its allotted share of bodies."

"That is correct." McKinnon is tight-lipped, disappointing the detective.

"Then the pandemic hit, and what happened?"

"Dad died."

"Your father passed, Marc Downsen was appointed coroner, and the rotation returned to the correct sequence. You lost a revenue stream."

"Correct. We struggled to make the payments on the note for the new crematorium and the processing lab. The Feds lied about the money."

Nearing the end of her questions, Carin uses the training and begins to tighten the interview with direct assertions.

"To compensate for the loss of revenue, you started making sure the McKinnon Funeral Home was the designation for people with stage IV cancers."

"Yes. That is a common marketing and sales strategy in our industry. The marketing premise is: *A plan now results in no worry later.*"

Breathing evenly, Carin closes the verbal noose.

"Killing people to accelerate your business cash flow is not found in common sales strategies."

"I didn't kill anyone. You got it wrong."

"We think we have it right. Motive. Ability. Intent. We have everything we need to build a case."

"You are wrong. Who do you think sent the emails?"

Stunned, Mojtabai and Trimble lean back at the same time. Jared McKinnon smiles his creepy grin for the first time.

"You didn't know. I assumed the Feds would be better — why else would I be here? I saw the holes in the bodies."

Mojtabai ignores the insult and lets Carin continue her questioning.

"You saw the bodies?"

"Yes, I am a licensed mortician. I can't afford to pay anyone else." McKinnon's admission confirmed that the chemical smell was mixing with his body odor. Carin ignores the invading funk and presses softly.

"I understand — business is slow, and funds are tight. What about the holes in the chests of the victims?"

"I knew something wasn't right with the bodies."

"What did you do?"

"I found the *Find the Slayer* forum on the internet. I created an anonymous account and started posting. Most people were just nuts. A few were serious about figuring out if the people were being murdered."

McKinnon stops speaking when he realizes he is dehydrated from the profuse sweating.

"Can I get some water?"

Without stopping the recordings, Carin rushes to the breakroom and returns with three paper cups of cool water. After guzzling the first cup, McKinnon continues.

"Thank you. Until you came along, Detective Trimble, no one outside the forum thought a serial killer was working the tri-county area."

"I had help. Figuring out a serial killer was active here was a team effort..." Carin's face flashes into unfiltered surprise at an internal revelation. McKinnon sees Carin's epiphany.

"Yep. Give the detective a prize. I gave Al the passwords. I sent Al the emails. I pointed him at you. I may go out of business. I may not have been financially prudent. You know that I am not a murderer. Someone is killing people for a reason we cannot determine."

"Who is we?"

"The forum. There are lots of theories — none hold water. The theory I like is too obvious."

Carin sits forward.

"Tell me anyway."

"Greene's pain trial is not going well. She has promised terminal patients no pain until the end. She's wrong with at least half the patients in the trial. I don't think Greene can accept the patients' suffering when she promised them an easy transition."

Carin taps her notepad with the pen while asking.

"You linked the victims to Dr. Greene and her pain trial?"

"I didn't make the connection. Someone in the forum

associated the victims with Greene's trial. The person posted a bogus access password to an EMR system, then vanished."

"EMR?"

"Electronic medical records."

"Bogus? How exactly did you get the password?"

"The person DM'd me with the password. I put the EMR password in one of the emails to Al."

Carin squints at McKinnon's statement and fights the urge to raise her voice.

"I have all the emails. There is no password."

"I knew it was illegal. In the note, I told Al to delete the email after copying the EMR password."

Using another interview technique, Carin changes to a complimentary line of questions.

"Jared, you seem to know a lot."

"It's Jared now? Whatever. It is still a small town."

"Yes, I suppose it is."

McKinnon sips another paper cup of water and turns to the FBI special agent.

"Agent Mojtabai, I thought the FBI would be doing the interrogation."

"Not everything you see on the television is accurate. Detective Trimble is doing a good job. Besides, this is not an interrogation — it is an interview. Which, by the way, is going well. Would you back up to the bodies you processed? What did you think of the wounds over the heart?"

Draining the second cup before he continues, Jared McKinnon has stopped pouring sweat.

"Do you know what a tire bead blaster is, Agent Mojtabai?"

"Enlighten me."

"A tire bead blaster is a compressed air tank. It is usually five gallons, handheld, and has a flattened nozzle and quick-release valve. Point the nozzle between the rim and the tire being mounted. Pull the release, and the rush of air inflates the tire enough to seal the bead."

"Thank you. Why are you telling us about a specialized tool?"

"Because what happened to the victims' hearts before the gun was used reminded me of a bead blaster."

"I don't follow."

"Agent, they sell compressed air in aerosol-type cans. Over-the-counter compressed air is used to clean everything, mainly electronics. The crumbs in your keyboard, for example. The cans are harmless unless you defeat the safety valve. Also, it's easy to make a miniature bead blaster with over-the-counter materials."

Downing the third cup of water, McKinnon likes being the focus of attention.

"What if. This is just speculation by me. What if someone created a smaller version of the bead blaster?"

Carin raises her shoulders and spine, adjusts her shirt, and then leans in.

"The earlier bodies. You knew they were murdered?"

"I thought the early victims might be murders. I spoke to your predecessor. He didn't want to hear my theory. He was ROAD."

Mojtabai shuffles in his seat because he doesn't like learning new things in an interview. Sucking in a breath, the special agent asks politely.

"Road?"

Carin responds to Mojtabai while staring at McKinnon.

"It is military acronym slang. Retired on active duty. R-O-A-D. Jared is telling us my predecessor was collecting a paycheck while not working on investigations. Jared?"

"Exactly right."

Carin makes a connection.

"Did you serve?"

"Navy. Ensign Mortician Jared McKinnon — Hooyah, Sergeant Trimble."

The fact that McKinnon knows she was discharged from the Marines raises her opinion of the greasy man. Carin wonders how someone with a military background can be frumpy. The financial pressures must be overwhelming for the former Navy Ensign. Pressing forward, the detective's questions become narrowly focused.

"Oorah. Jared, do you think Dr. Greene created a device that she used to explode the victims' hearts?"

"Yes."

"Okay. Do you have a theory as to why it went from a compressed air cannon-like device to something like a gun or small-caliber firearm?"

"No."

"You must have thought about the murders. Can you speculate?"

"The first device probably failed. The killer wanted something more reliable. Or maybe she modified the device."

"What do you mean?"

"Your teams didn't find any powder residue on the victims."

Mojtabai shuffles as Carin asks.

"That is not common knowledge. How did you know?"

"I didn't just inherit a business. I am a hands-on owner. I told you I processed the bodies. There were no powder marks. "

Returning to the nature of his heritage and what he learned from his immigrant parents, Mojtabai rocks his head side-to-side in agreement. Then, he leans in for his question.

"Speculate. Tell me how you think Greene created the device to kill people."

Holding up the empty cup, McKinnon waits for Carin to return with more water. After setting three new cups of water on the table, Carin's eyes flit to Mosh before she sits with a questioning expression. Jared sips and gives the detective and the special agent what they want.

"Again, this is speculation and imagination. I think it was simple to create the device. After Greene figured out how to defeat the safety valve, she adapted a pericardial needle to a can of compressed air. Stick the needle in the chest, pierce the heart, pull the trigger, and bam, exploded heart. I don't think she used a gun."

Mojtabai and Trimble look at each other and nod an

unspoken agreement before the special agent sits forward to speak.

"For the record, Jared McKinnon has been cooperative and forthcoming with information. Assuming Detective Trimble's concurrence, I will recommend that Mr. McKinnon receive a fine for defrauding the city of Marble Grove and the counties of Hemingway, Twekonda, and Juinera. Detective?"

"I concur."

"This ends the Jared Carol McKinnon interview."

Mojtabai presses the red button on the recording device. The monitor continues with an image of the room. The green light above the word "record" fades out.

"Are we off the record?"

Carin and Mojtabai both nod, and Carin answers.

"Yes, Jared. What do you want to say?"

"I tried to replicate the device. That is why I know so much. Here's the problem. Keeping the hose for the pericardial needle attached to the can is problematic. Releasing the rush of air, enough volume needed to cause damage, blows the hose off the can's nozzle. Unless Greene has more engineering and machinist skill than I imagine, I know why you think she switched to twenty-two shells."

Carin and Mojtabai wait, hoping, knowing McKinnon is not off the hook for the murders. Also, the investigators know McKinnon's speculation is not admissible. Maybe, just maybe, McKinnon can give them the clue they need to prove Greene is the murderer.

"She is not using pistol shells. That's why you didn't

find any gunpowder residue. She uses a frame to hold the needle to the can and position the jet of air."

Carin drinks the untouched water before her meek question.

"You think Greene created a bracket to hold the can of compressed air against the chest? The process was to insert the needle. Push the fabricated bracket, with the can of air, against the skin and the needle. The pressure of pushing the can onto the bracket releases the valve. Poof, compressed air is released, exploding the heart."

"That's about right. Greene could achieve the goal by using a bracket to hold the pericardial needle against the valve."

"Goal?"

"Detective Trimble, Greene's goal is to stop the pain her patients were experiencing."

"Go on."

"Remove the plastic tube and attach the pericardial needle directly to the pressure valve on the can of compressed air. Use the bracket to hold the needle in the correct place. Slam the device into the chest, release the air, and destroy the victim's heart. With one motion, the victims are no longer in pain."

"Anything else?"

"Isn't that enough?"

Pressing the intercom button, Carin dials.

"*Sergeant Kolston.*"

"Jan?"

"*Carin?*"

Grinning at the sergeant's tête-à-tête, Carin makes her request.

"Jan, please send a deputy to escort Mr. McKinnon out of the building."

"*Right away.*"

Carin presses the end call button, and McKinnon rises to wait for the escort.

"I'll pay the fines. Thank you. Both."

The door opens, and McKinnon leaves in silence. Excited, Carin is beaming with anticipation and spewing questions.

"Who gave up EMR access to the forum? Violating HIPAA could mean federal charges. We need to separate Greene and Mancone. Also —"

"Carin, slow down. Everything we got from McKinnon is speculation. Solid. Strong. Well-reasoned speculation. Do you want my suggestion?"

Duly chastised for her exuberance when caution is needed, Carin responds.

"You are the lead investigator."

"Cut Greene and Mancone loose. Stay the course. You know what you have to do. Will you do what is necessary? Making the hard choices is why they pay you."

Carin knows the special agent is teaching her another lesson. Accepting reality, she agrees.

"I think either Greene, Mancone, or someone who works with them gave up the EMR access. Mosh, I get it. Cut Greene and Mancone loose. Stay the course."

After pressing the intercom button, Carin dials.

"Sergeant Kolston."

"Jan, please send a deputy to escort Dr. Greene and Mrs. Mancone from the building.

"Right away."

"Also, please have Mrs. Demchuk brought to IR-B. Wait. Jan, you escort Mrs. Demchuk."

"On it."

Chapter Eighteen

Sitting across from Deena Demchuk in IR-B, Carin wonders how Deena's bouffant hairdo stays in place. The women of the fifties and sixties used a massive amount of ozone-depleting hair spray. Deena must use something to keep her hair piled high.

"Mrs. Demchuk, thank you for taking a few minutes to speak with us."

"You did all this. A woman shouldn't be a detective. Especially an inexperienced woman. Your predecessor would not have scared and worried my son like you have."

Mojtabai raises a palm and his trained investigator's voice.

"For the record, I am Special Agent Karim Mojtabai. With me is Detective Carin Trimble. The date and time of the video recording are accurate. We are interviewing Deena Clarin Demchuk. Mrs. Demchuk, do you live at 1901 South Marble Quarry Circle?"

"You know that is where I live. Why are you accusing my son of murder?"

"No one is accusing anyone of anything. We are trying to gather information. Mrs. Demchuk, can you tell us where you were the night Al was attacked?"

"Where was I? At home. Like always."

"Will Mr. Demchuk confirm you were home all evening?"

"John spends his time in the den, working on those stupid model trains. I could be dead for all he knows when he goes into the den."

"You are unable to verify you were home at the time Al was attacked?"

"What are you saying? You are no better than her."

Mojtabai refuses to take the bait from the irritating woman wearing too much makeup.

"I am just asking questions to create a picture of recent events."

Sliding a picture from a folder and spinning it for Mrs. Demchuk to scan, Mojtabai examines the woman's face for clues and receives a hint.

"Mrs. Demchuk, do you know this person?"

"That is Jared McKinnon Senior."

"That is correct. Who is Jared McKinnon Senior to you?"

"To me? Nobody."

"We have reason to believe that you and the elder Jared McKinnon were close and conducted a decades-long affair."

"Lies. It is all lies. This town is full of liars lying all the time."

Mojtabai is internally pleased his question annoyed the irritating Deena Demchuk.

"I am not going to dispute your premise about small-town gossip. I've been told there are some surprisingly good stories floating around. Stories based on gossip are not relevant to our immediate concern. Let's stick to the facts."

Sliding a second picture from a folder and spinning it for Mrs. Demchuk to scan, Mojtabai again focuses on Deena's face for clues. The sweat oozing through the makeup on the woman's forehead is a massive hint.

"That's not me."

"My team in Virginia says otherwise. I am sure you know the man standing behind you. The video shows you holding his hand and kissing him on the way out of the store."

"So what? Jared was nice to me. He paid attention to me. Jared loved me."

"I am sure he did, along with his wife and several other women."

"Jared loved me. He helped with Al."

"Is Al Jared's son?"

"No! Jared and I started seeing each other when Al was about eight — when my mother died."

Carin shuffles at the uncomfortable idea that the funeral home director preyed on grieving women. She leans her elbows on the table to change the tone of the interview.

"Your life, the milestones you remember, all tie back to Al. You have done a great job with Al."

Taken aback by the compliment from a woman she loathes, Deena nods a polite, silent thank you. Carin continues.

"Deena, when did you meet Jared McKinnon?"

"I knew who he was. We became close when my mother died."

"I see. Why did you buy a nailer?"

"The crew working on the upgrades to Al's apartment needed a nailer. I told them I'd buy a nailer and bring it to them if they kept working."

"Why was Jared McKinnon with you in the store?"

"Whenever I had an excuse to escape John, I called Jared. He often tagged along because he liked my company."

"And?"

"And what? It is true what they call you. Detective Know-Nothing. At least Kenny was smart enough to keep his mouth shut and stay out of other people's business."

Ignoring the insult and reference to her predecessor's corrupt nature, Carin remains even-tempered in tone and posture.

"What else did Jared do for you?"

"What else? You are sick. I will tell you what Jared did for me. He taught me sex. Real sex, not that stuff I learned from that peckerwood LeClare or in Louisiana. We did everything two people can do to each other, and I loved it all."

Surprised, Carin redirects Deena's responses.

"I am sorry, Mrs. Demchuk. I was not clear in my question. Did Jared, a trained pathologist, teach you about the human body? Did you and Jared McKinnon discuss how a body might react to different physical threats?"

The truculent Mrs. Deena Demchuk surprises the interviewers.

"I want a lawyer."

Mojtabai receives a confirmation nod from Carin, who closes the session.

"This is the end of the interview with Mrs. Demchuk. The date and time are confirmed accurate on the video."

Mojtabai presses the red button, ending the recording.

The monitor continues with an image of the room. Carin presses the intercom button and dials.

"*Sergeant Kolston.*"

"Jan, please send a deputy to escort Mrs. Demchuk to Holding Cell A. Make sure she has access to a phone."

"*Right away.*"

"You can't hold me! I am not under arrest."

"Mrs. Demchuk, we can hold you. When your attorney arrives, we'll resume the discussion."

Sergeant Kolston opens the interview room's door, and Carin repeats the order.

"Jan, please escort Mrs. Demchuk to Holding Cell A."

"On it."

* * *

Chief Johnston realizes that giving in to his nephew's insistence on observing his mother while being questioned was a mistake.

"Al, are you okay?"

"Yes. Uncle Myron, is Mom a bad person for what she did with Jared McKinnon?"

"No, Al. People do things all the time that others may or may not approve of as moral or ethical. It doesn't make them a bad person. It means they are human. People make mistakes. We don't stop loving them because they're flawed. Do you understand?"

"Yes. People make mistakes."

"Do you want to talk to your mom?"

"No."

"I understand this is tough for you. Do you want to go home?"

"Can I talk to Detective Carin?"

"Yes, of course."

* * *

"Hello, Chief. Al. What's up?"

"Carin, Al wanted to chat with you."

Reverting to his head-down nervous stance, Al points to the chief and Mojtabai. Both take the hint, eye Carin and then exit IR-A.

"Al, what's up?"

"I know where it is."

"Where what is?"

"The can."

"Al, what can?"

"The can with the needle."

Dumbfounded, Carin grasps that Al knows the location of the murder weapon.

"Al, stop talking. Please, this is important. I am going to call in the Chief and Agent Mojtabai. They need to hear what you are saying. Is that okay?"

"You and me. We solved the case."

"Yes, Al, you and me. Can I ask them to come in?"

"Yes."

Al sits across the table, refusing to look anywhere other than at the table. Carin knows her new friend is struggling to keep it together. Unnatural for the former Marine, something she knows is needed is a soft and caring tone.

"For the record, I am Detective Carin Trimble. Special Agent Karim Mojtabai and Chief Myron Johnston are with me. The date and time of the video recording are accurate. We are interviewing Marcus Alvin Demchuk. Mr. Demchuk, do you live at 1901 South Marble Quarry Circle?"

"A."

"Mr. Demchuk, do you live at 1901-*A* South Marble Quarry Circle?"

"Yes."

"Mr. Demchuk, are you speaking to us voluntarily?"

"Yes."

"Mr. Demchuk, for the Special Agent, the Chief, and the record, please tell us what you told me a few minutes ago."

"Al."

"*Al*, please tell us what you told me a few minutes ago."

"I know where it is."

"Please explain to me what you are referring to. What is it that you mentioned to me a few minutes ago."

"The can with the needle."

"Can you take us to the can with the needle?"

"Yes."

*** *** ***

"Al, for the camera, please confirm this is where you

live, 1901 South Marble Quarry Circle, and that we have your permission to enter."

"Detective Carin, I live here. We can go inside."

Al opens the front door and quickly presses the security code to his parents' home. Before they enter, John Demchuk pulls the door wide and waves the group forward. Entering, Carin trails Al, Mojtabai, and Chief Johnston. Two forensics team members, one pulling on gloves and the other videotaping the investigation trail the group.

The group follows in a line through the house, across the kitchen to the breakfast nook. Stopping at the table, Al points to the bench seat. Carin steps close to Al, who does not move away from someone stepping into his personal zone. Hesitating, Carin falls back on her training and PTSD therapy sessions. She is not fond of physical contact that is not intimate or martial arts sparring. The detective overcomes the hard lessons she received as a young girl from her mother. Deciding to go ahead, she gingerly places her hand on Al's shoulder before asking.

"Is the can with the needle in the storage under the bench?"

"Yes."

Carin gently pulls Al aside, allowing the forensics team to approach the nook. Pulling away the chairs and the table exposes the entire bench and storage compartment. Lifting the floral seat cushion and putting it on the table, the wooden lid of the storage compartment is revealed.

Carin notices Al's apartment through the window above the nook.

Her thoughts run dark, wondering if this is the day she destroys Al's idyllic life.

The forensic analyst wearing gloves moves to the side, creating an optimal video image, before lifting the lid. Using exaggerated movements for the camera, she lifts the cover to the compartment in a smooth motion. Inside are several plastic storage bins. The gloved analyst looks to Carin, who asks her partner for guidance.

"Which bin is it in?"

"It's not in a bin."

"Is it not here?"

"It is under the boxes."

The gloved analyst moves the three bins, stacking them on the floor just outside the nook, then looks to Al for guidance.

"Look under."

Peering in and then waving forward the analyst who is taping, more light in the compartment reveals a strap. Pulling on the tab raises a false bottom in the storage bench. Waiting for the video tech to nod and confirm she has covered every inch of the hidden compartment with the video, the gloved analyst reaches down to retrieve an oversized tin cash box.

Chapter Nineteen

"For the record, I am Special Agent Karim Mojtabai. With me is Detective Carin Trimble. The location, date, and time of the video recording are accurate. We are resuming the interview with Deena Clarin Demchuk. Attorney Theodore Monroe is present to represent Mrs. Demchuk."

Using gloved hands to open a sizeable beige evidence bag, Carin places the tin box on the table before Mojtabai continues.

"Mrs. Demchuk, is this container familiar to you?"

"My client exercises her Fifth Amendment right against self-incrimination."

"I'd like to hear that from Mrs. Demchuk."

After looking at her attorney, remembering their rehearsal, and getting a nod, Deena parrots the message from her attorney.

"I invoke my Fifth Amendment right."

"We found this container in your home. Can you tell us how this cash box came to be in the storage under the breakfast nook bench?"

"I invoke my Fifth Amendment right."

Mojtabai points. Carin pulls a second beige evidence bag closer and opens it to expose the contents. With a stiff face, she draws a large spray can from the envelope. Still in their packaging, several pericardial needles follow the spray can onto the table. Lifting a third piece of evidence from the stack, Detective Trimble places its contents next to the needles. The wire and steel component appears to have no purpose until Carin slides it close to the spray can. Carin moves a fourth evidence bag near the table's edge, leaves it sealed, and comments.

"Deena, the scrubs you wore are in that bag. Mosh?"

Attorney Monroe barks.

"That is speculation."

Mojtabai rocks his head side-to-side in agreement, then continues.

"Mrs. Demchuk, can you tell us about these devices?"

"I invoke my Fifth Amendment right."

"Mrs. Demchuk, how did these devices get into the cash box and into the storage bin under the bench in your kitchen?"

"I invoke my Fifth Amendment right."

Shifting his pleather-covered folio closer and tapping the FBI logo for effect, Special Agent Karim Mojtabai opens the folio and looks over his list of questions.

"Mrs. Demchuk, I have at least sixty questions on these pages. We can run the list and get your response, invoking the Fifth, for all sixty questions. Then we can start again. Or, I have a better idea. We can put you in the holding cell and resume tomorrow after Detective Trimble and I create more questions. Mr. Monroe, I think we are finished for today."

Pressing the intercom button, Carin dials the duty sergeant and begins putting the evidence back into their reinforced paper containers while issuing orders.

"*Sergeant Kolston.*"

"Jan, please send a female deputy to escort Mrs.

Demchuk to a holding cell and an escort for Mr. Monroe to leave the building."

"Right away."

Mojtabai closes his folio, pushes back, and begins to rise — fully knowing Deena Demchuk doesn't want the social stigma of the neighbors gossiping about her spending the night in jail.

"It's not mine. Have you spoken to Sharon Greene?"

Carin looks to Mojtabai and then continues to close the evidence bags. The psychological win gives Carin a thin smile, which she hides by placing the evidence bag on the floor. Mojtabai waits for Carin to sit up and refocus before asking.

"I know, that you know, from the news reports that we have spoken to several people regarding the recent homicides. You told us the box is not yours. That leaves a question. Whose murder weapon is it?"

Monroe holds his hand in front of his client with his comment.

"You don't know that is a murder weapon."

"Not yet. Mrs. Demchuk, whose are the items we showed you?"

"I have no idea. I'm sure Sharon Greene, or that pretty PA, might have something to say about these things."

"Why were the devices hidden in your storage bin?"

"I have no idea. Someone is trying to blame me for the deaths of those people."

Mosh doesn't look away from Deena.

"How did your son, Al, know the items were in the cash

box hidden under the false bottom of the storage bench?"

"I have no idea. Did you ask Al?"

Monroe leans in, and Carin chimes before he can speak on his client's behalf.

"Thank you, Mrs. Demchuk. We have what we need for today. We will resume tomorrow afternoon at 1:30. Is that okay with everyone?"

Nods from Mojtabai, Deena, and Monroe confirm Carin's request just as Sergeant Kolston and a female deputy enter the interview room.

"Jan, change of plan. Please escort Mrs. Demchuk and Mr. Monroe from the building."

"Right away."

The interview room door closes, leaving Carin with Mojtabai, who leans forward to end the recording and then sits back and waits.

"Mosh, I keep returning to something the Chief stated a few weeks ago. '*Al is no dummy.*' What if Mom is willing to take the fall for her son?"

"Thin. Possible. On day one, I told you to write Al's name on the whiteboard. Here's another idea."

"Hold that thought. Mosh, let's get lunch and chat."

* * *
** ** **

"Carin, smart move. We don't know if the chief was monitoring the interview room. It looks like rain is possible. Is sitting outside a good idea?"

"It's not going to rain. Besides, what's life without a

little suspense?"

"You like this café."

"I like this place. It has good food and good people. Isn't that sandwich tasty? Also, they make a great meatless burger. Mosh, we have a problem."

"Who's we, Kemosabe?"

"You watched too much television as a kid. Mosh, you are on point for this cluster. I'm just the gopher. We have to interview Al and the Chief. Also, we cut them loose. I think we need to revisit Greene and Mancone. A second round of questions could lead to something."

"Just Al."

"You must be the FBI." Marg Lyttle stepped to the side of the table, her rear too close to the seated Carin's face for comfort.

"Hello. I am Special Agent Karim Mojtabai. You are?"

"Carin didn't tell you? I am Marg Lyttle. L-Y-T-T-L-E. I wanted to introduce myself and let you know I am available if you need information or anything."

Stepping close to the sitting Mosh, Marg makes everyone uncomfortable.

"Anything at all, I am a phone call away. Carin knows where I live. She can direct you — you know, if you want to have tea or something."

"Thank you for the offer. I'll keep it in mind."

"I am just letting you know that *something* is on the table. I'm off to visit an old friend. Toodle-Doodle." Waiting for Marg, the busybody, to be out of earshot, Mosh restarts the discussion.

"What was that?"

"I think the local busybody has eyes for the new guy. You said, *'Just Al'*?" Carin is happy when Mojtabai ignores Marg's interruption.

"I ran the chief's finances and credit cards. He and his wife were away when two of the murders occurred. Also, he has no unusual transactions on his bank and credit card history. Although, his wife has some family money."

"Were you going to tell me you ran a parallel investigation?"

"Not parallel, and yes, when the time came, I'd tell you. The time is here. You know why I didn't tell you about looking into the Chief."

"You know, I'd have done it — looked into the Chief. I understand why you didn't tell me."

"Now you can say you didn't investigate the guy who promoted you to detective. Stick it on me if anything goes sideways. Your friend Al, is he able to stand up to questioning?"

Carin downs a forkful of salad, sips unsweetened tea, thinks, and then looks at her new friend with concern.

"What about Greene and Mancone?"

"We can talk to them. However, our focus should be on Al."

"I agree. I don't want Al to be the murderer. Understood, we must follow all the leads. He knew everything, far more than what was in McKinnon's emails. He knew where the murder weapon was and took us right to it."

Carin looks up and presses the investigation lead.

"What do you think?"

"I think you didn't answer my question. Will your friend Al stand up to questioning?"

"If we… if I ask the questions in the right way, with the right tone, Al will respond well. If he gets nervous or agitated, we'll have to stop and start again after he calms down. It may take a while. Yes, I think we can interview Al."

"Carin, what are the other options?"

Taken aback at Mojtabai's question, Carin slowly, methodically, reviews the case and the process that led her to this moment at a sidewalk café. Looking up from her internal frustration, a lightning-bolt idea screams at the new detective as she spots the ASD facility down the street.

"We can use Laura."

"Laura? The woman with speech disabilities?"

"Yes. Laura and Al have a relationship. I think they have a relationship. Anyway, they have known each other since childhood. He is a different person around her. Al will respond well to Laura asking questions."

Mosh is evaluating the idea aloud.

"How? I mean, it's a good idea. Normally, we'd get her to wear a wire and ask the correct questions. Didn't I read — did you tell me they communicate through texts? It will take a few days to get a warrant and set up the mirrors to trap their texts."

"We don't need a warrant or the mirroring."

"Why not?"

"Because Laura and Al are good people. We tell them

what we are doing and use the recording in an interview room to document the interaction."

"Back up. Carin, what's in your head that I'm missing?"

Beaming, pushing away the nearly empty salad bowl, Carin knows her detective skills are on point.

"I learned a lot at the Pritchett Center for Autism. The brochures they gave me were helpful. Al's quirks drift away into the breeze when he exchanges texts with Laura. We will give Laura a list of simple, short, quickly texted questions that she can easily key into her phone. Al will focus on responding using the speech-to-text application, or he can respond verbally. Laura's not deaf. We'll get it all on the video. Here's the best part."

Mojtabai drains his chai tea, evaluating the bombshell idea from his new friend.

"Mosh, we'll make it a group text."

Mojtabai takes a long time to consider the legal implications of Carin's idea to use Laura and a group chat to interview a murder suspect. Trimble sees the angst forming in Mojtabai and cuts off the complaint before he tries to end the problematic approach before it begins.

"With Al's condition, we'll never get a conviction to stick. We can get him to tell us why he did it and then decide what we want to do with the information."

"Why do you think he did it?"

Taken aback at the semi-tangential question, Carin ponders before responding.

"I have no idea."

** ** **

"For the record, I am Special Agent Karim Mojtabai. Detective Carin Trimble and Miss Tawni Laura-Mara Pritchett are with me. The location, date, and time of the video recording are accurate. We are interviewing Marcus Alvin Demchuk. Attorney Theodore Monroe is present to represent Mr. Demchuk.

"Thank you all for agreeing to meet. As you know, we prepared a series of questions for Mr. Demchuk. Mr. Monroe, do you have any concerns with our questions?"

"Not at this time."

"Mr. Monroe, do you have any concerns about the approach we created to communicate our questions?"

"Not at this time."

"Mr. Demchuk, do you have any concerns with the process we outlined?"

"Al."

"I am sorry. Al, do you have any concerns with the process we outlined?"

Al mimics his attorney.

"Not at this time."

"Miss Pritchett, are you okay to proceed?"

Laura signs yes — her hand a fist bobbing vertically.

"For the record, Miss Pritchett has signed yes. Detective Trimble?"

Carin responds to the special agent's order by grabbing the cable that stretches across the table. The far end of the cord is inserted into the video recording machine.

Connecting the USB-C end of the line to her phone, the text message application appears as a pop-up in the corner of the room's video image.

> **Laura-Mara**
> Al?

>> **Al Demchuk**
>> Hi Laura.

> **Laura-Mara**
> Hi Al.

Looking around the room at the faces that are looking back, Mojtabai doesn't perceive a negative vibe.

"Shall we proceed? Detective Trimble will guide the interview. Miss Pritchett, please begin with question one on the list."

> **Laura-Mara**
> Al, do you know why we are here?

>> **Al Demchuk**
>> To find the murderer.

Carin lets Laura type the following question, then gently places her hand on Laura's.

"Al, Laura can hear you. If it is okay with Laura, you can speak your answers."

Laura signs yes — her hand a fist bobbing vertically, while smiling at Al with raised eyebrows. Carin nods for Laura to continue, and the woman presses the send arrow.

Laura-Mara
How did you know the device was hidden in the cash box?

"I saw it."
Carin is gentle with her guidance.
"Laura, please skip to question four."

Laura-Mara
Did you see who put the cash box under the bench?

"No."

Laura-Mara
Did you put the cash box under the bench?

"No."

"Laura, please skip to question nine." Carin's tone receives a smile from the attorney, allowing her to continue. Because texting is Laura's primary form of communication, her fingers flawlessly fly over the tiny digital keyboard. Carin and Mosh have inserted Al-friendly verbiage into the list of questions.

Laura-Mara
When did you first see the cash box?

"A long time ago."

Carin again places her hand on Laura's, requesting the woman wait.

"Al, was it a week, a month, a year, or more when you first saw the cash box under the storage bench?"

Detective Carin's question causes Al to twitch and shuffle in his chair. He looks to Carin, smiles at Laura, and then returns to a heads-down focus on his phone. Carin realizes her question is out of line for Al.

"It was a long time."

> **Laura-Mara**
> *A long time ago?*

Carin corrects herself, knowing she must keep Laura as Al's focus. She won't make the mistake again.

"Laura, please skip to question eleven."

> **Laura-Mara**
> *How come you didn't tell Detective Carin about the cash box sooner?*

Al doesn't respond. Everyone waits, unsure, until Laura types an impromptu text.

> **Laura-Mara**
> *Al? I am your friend. Tell me so we can help. I will help you.*
>> **Al Demchuk**
>> *I saw it.*

Laura-Mara
We know you saw it. How come you didn't tell Detective Carin about the cash box?

Al Demchuk
Too much pain.

Laura looks to Carin for help. Everyone in the room is confused by Al's response. Not knowing the correct approach, Carin decides on an alternate method.

"Partner, may I ask you a question?"

Al Demchuk
Yes.

"Remember when we talked about being partners?"

Al Demchuk
Yes.

"Partner, you don't have to send text responses to me." Carin pushes her partner to answer.

"Is that okay?"

"Yes."

"Good. Thank you. What did we say about partners?"

"We agreed. Partners share information."

"Exactly right. Is there anything you want to tell me?"

Al looks at Laura with sadness washing over his face, causing Laura's fingers to fly over her phone. Carin, Mosh, and Theodore are riveted on the monitor and the picture-in-picture image of the texts.

> **Laura-Mara**
> *I am your friend. Tell me so I can help.*
> *No matter what you did, I will still love*
> *you.*

"You love me?"

> **Laura-Mara**
> *Yes, and you know it. Don't play ASD*
> *with me. I know your games.*

Called out by someone who knows him too well, the color returns to Al's face and a brightness to his eyes. Laura and Al are beaming at each other. Al refuses to look away, and Laura accepts his stare — until he speaks.

"I love you too."

> **Laura-Mara**
> *Al, tell them what you know. After we*
> *are done with the questions, we can*
> *walk. I like our walks.*

"I like our walks too. They will put me in jail."

Laura looks around the room in a panic. Signing the word "no," snapping two fingers against her thumb, she is mouthing the word "no" with each snap. Carin lays her hand flat between Laura and Al.

"We are not putting Al in jail. We are here to discover

what happened and how Al learned those items were hidden in the cash box. Laura, move to question sixteen, please."

Carin accepts the knowing smile from Mojtabai, who knows the no jail comment is thin. Mojtabai knows the detective is using Laura and the texts to put Al back in a comfortable position.

Laura-Mara
Who put the box under the bench?

Theodore, the attorney, growls at the pop-up box on the video monitor.

"Follow the rules, or we are done here."

Carin's tone defuses Attorney Ted's intended tension.

"Al, you don't have to answer that question. Laura, you have to ask the questions as they are written. Please, ask number sixteen again."

"You can ask."

"What's that, Al?

"Detective Carin, you can ask the questions."

"Al, are you sure? Laura wants to help. Should we let her help?"

"Laura is my friend. You are my friend. I will answer your questions."

"Thank you. That's good news. Al, do you know who put the items in the cash box and hid it under the bench?"

"Yes."

"Please tell us who hid the cash box under the bench."

Carin ignores Attorney Ted's glare.

"I did."

Ted leans closer to speak.

"Al, you do not have to say anything. I am asking you not to say anything else. Do you understand?"

"I understand. The wrong side of a pissing contest is never good."

Carin enlightens the others in the room.

"Al paraphrased a line from Mark Bello's *Betrayal in Blue*. Please tell us, *partner*, why you hid the cash box under the bench."

After a long moment, Al speaks while admiring Laura's face.

"To help another... Sometimes, a man must do things he does not want or desire."

"Al, what does that mean?"

"Detective Carin, I want to go home now."

Shuffling in her seat and noting Mojtabai is also squirming, Carin calls an executive audible.

"Special Agent Mojtabai has to approve. You should be able to go home. Al, you must promise to come back tomorrow and speak with us. Talk to me tomorrow. Is that a deal, partner?"

"It is a deal. Laura, will you walk with me?"

Laura-Mara

Al, it is a long way home from here to your house. Detective Carin will take me home. Is that okay?

"Laura, if you want to walk with Al, text me when you're ready to go home, and I'll come and get you. I am happy to give you a ride. Al, is that okay with you?"

"Yes."

"Laura?"

Laura-Mara
I will text you.

Mojtabai leans forward, positions his finger, and then speaks before pressing the button to end the recording.

"This ends the Marcus Alvin Demchuk interview."

Chapter Twenty

Case ID :	A-116
Name of Deceased :	Robert Carol McKinnon
Date of Report :	16-Sep-23
Cause of Death :	A gunshot to the head.
Place of Death :	1787 N Marble Quarry Cir
Date of Death :	15-Sep-23
Time of Death :	21:00-22:00
Investigator :	Marcus Alvin Demchuk

Background

The victim lives at home, alone.

Details

1)
2)
3)

"Deputy, is that camera on?" Carin's tartness does not go unnoticed.

"It is always on. A detective should know police body cameras are always active. Detective, are you okay?"

"Come with me. Keep me in the camera. Don't say

anything. Just record the interaction."

"Sure. Why?"

"There is a suspect in a murder investigation here. I need to get him away from the scene."

The deputy accepts Carin's orders, then follows her onto the vast porch of 1787 North Marble Quarry Circle.

"You can't be here." Stepping closer into his personal space, Carin knows it will upset Al.

"Detective Carin, I have the report." Al is almost pleading with the detective.

"Thank you. You can stay if you move to the sidewalk and stand with others. That deputy over there is rolling out the boundary tape. Please stand on the other side of the yellow tape. This deputy will escort you to the sidewalk."

Al accepts the order from his partner and moves to the other side of the neon yellow boundary. The deputy pulled the Police Line Do Not Cross tape and waited for Al before closing the loop. Mari and Ash emerge from their response vehicle with an empty gurney and proceed to the porch.

"Good morning, Detective Trimble." Mari is joyous.

"Good morning, Mari. Ash."

Ash, of course, is unable to remain quiet.

"What happened?"

"Come with me. Leave the gurney on the porch until the forensics people give you the okay to remove the body. Put on your booties and gloves. I'll wait."

Booties and gloves ready, Ash enters the hundred-year-old home and ascends the narrow stairs — following Mari, who trails Carin. Ash is sure Mari admires Carin climbing the stairs. Uncharacteristically, he says nothing. Turning left into the main bedroom, the trio passes a deputy standing guard in the narrow hallway. Carin's thoughts are darker than she wants.

"Half of Marble Grove's on-duty force is at this call. Entering, they find the room covered in a pink hue."

"Look up. Don't let his brains drip on you." Again, Ash is unable to constrain himself. Ignoring the insensitive twenty-something, Carin leans closer to the bed, and the body clothed only in blood-spattered tighty-whities. The detective forces herself to speak in a soft voice.

"This was Jared McKinnon. Mari, what do you see?"

Carin wants opinions. Before Mari can answer, Mojtabai enters the room and stands to the side. Carin accepts Fed's nod before returning to Mari for input. Mari tilts her head and begins to answer Carin's request for analysis.

"The victim sat on the edge of the bed. That pistol is an XCRD .45-caliber 1911 model. Over there, in the corner, is the other half of his skull. Jared knew how to do it right — this was no half-assed attempt hoping for sympathy. I saw something like this in the barracks over in Kunduz Province."

Mari pauses, giving Carin time to calculate dates. She realizes she was in Kunduz Province a couple of years before Mari entered the Army. Mari continues, leaning closer to read the writing impressed into the base of the discharged shell lying on the duvet.

"That shell case is a Martin Ranger One. It was ejected, bounced off that wall, and landed on the bedcover. Based on the dispersal, my guess is that the rounds are hollow points with an exit velocity close to 2k."

"Come on, 2,000 feet per second with a .45-caliber handgun? No way. That is way fast for a 1911 type." Ash interrupted his partner. Mari continued her summary without a hint of frustration at being questioned by the inexperienced EMT.

"The new model pistols are hand cannons designed to handle higher velocities. Carin, your forensics people will confirm what I see. Why are you asking me for something you already know, and your team will confirm?"

"All information is good information. You've seen more gunshot wounds than probably all of Hemingway County combined. You and Ash, wait in the hall for forensics."

"You've probably seen as many GSWs as I have." Carin chooses not to respond to Mari's statement. Mojtabai steps forward when Ash and Mari exit and stand down the hall.

"That EMT wants to talk to you about something."

"Who?"

"Mari." Carin ignores the comment.

"Why would McKinnon kill himself?"

"Oh, we're going to ignore the vibe? Okay. You invited her opinion because you like hearing her talk. Why would McKinnon kill himself? Which of the top reasons for suicide fits best? Jealousy? Maybe. Money troubles? Probably. Both? Maybe. Mental problems? Possible. Maybe it's an all-in deal because Jared McKinnon was overwhelmed. I don't see a note, do you?"

"No note yet. Wait! Come with me." After another

glance around the room, Carin agrees with the special agent. Rushing past the deputy, Mari, and Ash, racing down the stairs, and exiting the house, Carin and Mojtabai stop on the porch to yank off booties and gloves. Mojtabai follows Carin to the sidewalk, and Al.

"Come with us."

Following the order, Al shadows Mojtabai and his partner into the front room of the house, where Carin stands too close for Al's comfort.

"Did Jared McKinnon send you an email yesterday or last night?"

"Yes." Without being prompted, Al opens his phone, finds his email application, and forwards the McKinnon email. Carin's phone chimes immediately.

Opening the email, with Mojtabai looking over her shoulder, they read the note from Jared McKinnon.

Al,

Thank you for all your help. You have done a great job in a difficult situation. I want you to know that I loved your mother. I loved her more than I have loved anyone. When my father died, your mother came to me with help and understanding.

It broke Deena's heart when you saw us that day. I hope you can forgive me for creating problems between your parents. Deena and I never wanted to hurt you or your father. We never wanted to hurt anyone. Love is powerful. We had too much love for each other. Too much of anything leads to bad decisions.

Your mother and I made some bad decisions. Al, she loves you, and I would never have intentionally done anything to hurt you or your mother.

Tomorrow, a lot of information will be revealed. I think you already know what is coming. I know that you figured it out months ago. Despite what has happened, you can trust doctors. Do not let the actions of one doctor keep you from getting help when you need it. It was clever of you to take my advice and go to Detective Trimble.

Never let anyone tell you that you are not intelligent and wise. You are one of the most brilliant people I know. Ignore your mother. Marry Laura and live a good life.

With Love,
Jared

Mojtabai looks to Al, who is looking down, then turns to Carin, expecting her to speak. The detective uses a low volume and sweet tone with her partner. "You found out your mother and Mr. McKinnon were having an affair."

"Yes."

"What else did you learn about Mr. McKinnon and your mother?"

"Listen."

Mojtabai and Trimble wait for Al to resume.

"That is a scarlet tanager and an American goldfinch."

"The birds are nice. The other is the eastern bluebird."

Beaming, Al eyes his partner.

"You learned!"

"Yes, I learned. I like the bird songs and how much you know about birds. Right now, you need to help me. Partner, can you help me? What else did you learn about Mr. McKinnon and your mother?"

"Mom helped Dr. Greene."

** ** **

"For the record, I am Special Agent Karim Mojtabai. Detective Carin Trimble and Deena Clarin Demchuk are with me. Mr. Theodore Monroe is present to represent Mrs. Demchuk. Thank you all for agreeing to meet. Mrs. Demchuk, we have quite a few questions. Is there anything you'd like to say before we begin?"

"You canceled our meeting when Jared McKinnon blew his brains into the ceiling. It has been three weeks since you last interviewed my client. Nothing has changed. My client will not comment at this time. Mrs. Demchuk invokes Section Three of the Fifth Amendment."

"Thank you, Mr. Monroe. Detective Trimble, do you have a question?"

Carin and Mojtabai anticipated Deena Demchuk's attitude of superiority would force her to answer their questions. Shuffling to sit tall, her crisp white shirt taken

236

out of the dry cleaner bag for the interview, Carin is ready.

"Mrs. Demchuk, I have a short video to present."

Carin links her department-issued laptop to the video cable and presses play. The video image switches to a grainy black-and-white recording of a hooded figure in a hallway. Stopping before a door, the person tucks a package under her arm and pulls on gloves before entering room 118 of the Guardian Heart Hospice.

"Mrs. Demchuk, this video was recorded on the day Tercia Marie LeClare died. The person entered the room and found Miss LeClare had passed."

"That is speculation."

Carin doesn't miss a beat.

"Yes, Mr. Monroe, it is speculation. The person entered the room and *presumably* found Miss LeClare had passed, then quickly exited. The person leaves the room and exits the building via the emergency door at the end of the hall."

"So what?" Carin's eyes twinkle at Deena Demchuk's outburst, and she coolly continues.

"Please note that the emergency door is not fully closed. This person is me entering the room."

The video shows nothing for several long seconds. Carin resumes the narration with a matter-of-fact quality in her voice.

"The hooded figure re-enters through the emergency exit and moves directly into room 118. The person in the hoodie is surprised, *presumably*, to find me in the room and strikes me on the side of the head. Please note, the hooded figure is carrying something in their right hand."

A few seconds of a grainy hallway feels like minutes to the people watching. With a lilt in her voice, Carin continues her narration.

"Now the person is running away, again through the emergency exit. This person is your son Al, entering room 118. I'll pause. Mrs. Demchuk, do you have anything you want to say?"

"I invoke my Fifth Amendment right."

"Very well. I have another version of the video. Special Agent Mojtabai requested and received priority enhancement processing for the video. As you can see, the graininess is gone, the image is much more precise, and we can zoom in on various parts."

Carin waits for the right moment to stop the video.

"This is when the hooded person stops outside room 118, puts on the gloves, and enters the LeClare suite."

Attorney Monroe unconsciously leans closer to the video image. Mrs. Demchuk stares at the wall and the cheap print of trees surrounding a lake. Noting the frame is securely screwed to the wall, reminding her she is in an interrogation room, Deena Demchuk is becoming annoyed.

Mojtabai watches Demchuk for clues and sees the pulse quicken in the suspect's neck and her eyes darting from face to face. Carin takes a moment, breathes, and then zooms the image to the hands of the hooded figure using the touchpad on her PC.

"Is that your ring in the image, Mrs. Demchuk?"

"I invoke my Fifth Amendment right." Deena is defiant. Mosh interrupts.

"That is enough for today. We will resume tomorrow at nine."

Mosh pressing the button to end the recording triggers Deena and Ted to rise and leave. Carin chimes.

"Make sure you sign out at the front desk."

Ted turns his shoulders to nod understanding. Carin and Mosh wait for the door to close. Before she can speak, Mosh gives the order.

"Carin, go home. Get a good sleep. We can do this tomorrow."

"Why?" Carin is almost pleading.

"Look at your hands. I have never seen you sweat. Look down. We can do this tomorrow."

Carin refuses to look because she knows she has sweated through her shirt. Pressing her hands together, interlocking her fingers, and looking at Mosh, Carin refuses to acknowledge that her hands are shaking.

Chapter Twenty-One

Carin skipped zapping breakfast. Her stomach still aches from waking up and heaving. Retching becomes dry heaves when throwing up hard for so long that nothing is left to hurl. It had been a couple of years since she had the nightmare. She thought the recurring night horror was gone. It came back with a vengeance.

Brushing her hair, letting her coffee grow cold, and eyeing the new worry lines in the mirror, the detective's mind flashed to Kunduz Province.

Her orders were for Sergeant Carin Trimble and Corporal Janet Longmyer to arrest a marine whose CO found heroin in his gear. She'd done it dozens of times. Fly out and put the cuffs on a marine in a forward observation post. Load back into the Helo and unload at home base in an hour.

The LZ is next to the foxholes that ring a rise in the desert and create the forward location. This time, the Helo was a signal. When the skids touched the sand, the Helo began taking fire, so the pilot ordered Carin and Janet out before he lifted off to stand off and wait. Surrounded, the Marines expected their position to be overrun. Instead, the CO, Captain Bassington, deployed his troops, including the female MPs, in a defensive ring.

Carin and Janet jumped into a foxhole whose occupant nodded, grunted, and then jumped up and ran to join his buddy in another foxhole. Carin remembers fist-bumping Janet when she heard the CO call in air support. Pushing up the sandbags and checking the spare ammo magazines are stacked and within reach, Carin and Janet are ready. The CO went from marine to marine with one sentence for each person.

"Fight or die."

All voices hollered when the CO reached the last marine and returned to the center of the defensive perimeter.

"Oorah!"

"Oorah!"

"Oorah!"

Automatic weapons fire muffled the last Oorah and ushered death. In her mind, Carin sees Janet Longmyer's blood-soaked body. In the center of the ring, captain Bassington had been cut in half. Smoke rises from three locations where the airstrike pounded the ground. Looking around, knowing the Helo is landing, four more marines are gone. The marine they were there to arrest did not feel pain when the enemy bullet exploded his head.

Breathing deeply and focusing on her face in the mirror, Carin remembers the tools she learned in therapy.

"Why did the memory invade my dreams today?

"Because, today, I will destroy a family and send someone to prison.

"Probably to die in prison.

"My mind is playing games.

"I am doing the right thing.

"People deserve what they get when they are evil."

"I invoke my Fifth Amendment right." Deena is defiant.

"Very well. The analysis of the video is, of course, speculative. However, let me read the results from the report." Carin is focused.

> "Analysis of the nail polish color concludes it is consistent with being in the red palette spectrum and is found in commonly available products. Testing indicates the color is likely *Joyful Fear* or *Reckless Red*."

"Mrs. Demchuk, the new AI forensic tools are rarely flawed. Color accuracy doesn't matter. Out of curiosity, what is the name of the nail color you are wearing right now?"

"I invoke my Fifth Amendment right."

"We questioned John, your husband, about your fashion choice. You only have one color of nail polish. Is that correct, Mrs. Demchuk?"

About to answer, Deena holds her tongue, then continues when Ted Monroe puts his hand on her forearm.

"I invoke my Fifth Amendment right."

"For the record, John Demchuk confirmed Deena Demchuk uses *Joyful Fear* nail polish. The ring in the image is the ring you are wearing right now. Is that correct, Mrs. Demchuk?"

"That is speculation."

"No, Mr. Monroe, it is not speculation. We will confirm the photogrammetric measurement of the diamonds in Mrs. Demchuk's ring for size and relative location in the mounting. As you can see, the ring is unique. We will prove that the ring in the security video image is the ring she is wearing."

"Special Agent Mojtabai, I thought the FBI was running this investigation?"

"I don't understand your question, Mr. Monroe — I am sitting right here."

"Why are you letting this woman slander my client?"

"Slander? Are you sure that is the word you want to use? *Accuse* might be a better choice, given the evidence."

Realizing he has overstepped, Attorney Monroe turns his fight back to Detective Trimble.

"Detective, where are you going with these questions?"

Sitting tall, pulling her shirt tight, Detective Carin Trimble has waited her entire career for this moment.

"I am going to switch videos. What you are seeing is the enhanced video from the doorbell camera that captures the moment Al Demchuk was struck in the head. One moment. I will read the analysis results."

"With a 97.7% confidence, photogrammetry analysis confirms the assailant in the video is the same person in the Guardian Heart Hospice video."

"You may not be aware of the term. The definition for photogrammetry is the process of determining reliable dimensions of an object from photographs. Deena Clarin Demchuk, I am arresting you for assault."

"Stupid bitch."

"Deena, I am telling you, shut up."

"No, Ted. This woman has no idea what she is doing. What did Kenny call you in the interview? Detective-Know-Nothing. You have no idea what we did to help those people."

"Deena, please. I am telling you, stop talking."

"No, Ted, I will not shut up."

Mojtabai stands, forcing everyone to look at him before speaking. Mosh firmly wants to protect the case and prevent legal problems at a trial.

"We are going to recess for fifteen minutes. Mrs. Demchuk, I strongly urge you to speak with your attorney and take his advice seriously. Carin?"

Pressing the intercom button, Carin dials the duty sergeant.

"Sergeant Kolston."

"Jan, please send a deputy to escort Mrs. Demchuk and Mr. Monroe from IR-A to Holding Cell A. They need some privacy."

"Holding Cell A is occupied."

"Yes, of course. Have Dr. Greene brought to IR-A."

"On it."

Mojtabai presses the red button on the recording device and confirms that the monitor is recording.

Deena blurts while rising to exit.

"You are going to talk to Sharon? That bitch is clueless. Ask her how much she gets paid for that pain trial that doesn't work."

The proper Mrs. Demchuk, one of Marble Grove's self-appointed elites, has reverted to the rough-and-tumble woman she was after returning from Louisiana. Living a couple of years with her hard-scrabble relatives in the South stiffened the fierce woman's personality. It made her more willing to create a scuffle.

"Deena! Shut up!"

"Fuck it and fuck you, Ted. You didn't tell me to shut up when I was slurping on your business. Jared told me you were useless. He was right."

The door opens with the escort deputy entering — interrupting Deena's tirade. With tight grins, Carin and Mosh watch the deputy, Deena, and Ted exit the interrogation room. Mojtabai leans across, ends the recording, and then chimes with his native accent rolling effortlessly across the words.

"I think prissy Mrs. Deena Demchuk has secrets."

"No one with that hairstyle and *Joyful Fear* on her nails would live a double life." Carin's humor is not ignored.

"Ha! I don't think I've heard sarcasm from you."

* * *
** ** **

The deputy enters and guides Dr. Greene to a seat. Mojtabai presses several sequences on the control panel for the recording device. Satisfied he has made the correct adjustments, the special agent turns and smiles at the people in IR-A.

"For the record, I am Special Agent Karim Mojtabai.

Detective Carin Trimble and Dr. Sharon Greene are with me.

"Thank you all for agreeing to meet. Dr. Greene, we have a few questions. Is there anything you'd like to say before we begin?"

"Call me Sharon, and I have no questions."

With a raised eyebrow, Carin recognizes Dr. Greene is attempting to soften her image. Missing is this week's neon hair color. The new hair color is something found in nature, a classic brunette hue. The doctor is pressing the flattop into a softer style. Carin opens the discussion with a compliment.

"Thank you, Sharon. You changed your hair. It's nice."

"Thank you."

"You are not under arrest. We would like to ask you several questions. If at any time, however, you become uncomfortable, we can stop, and you can retain an attorney."

"Why would I need an attorney?"

"As you know, we are conducting a murder investigation. You have been implicated."

"Implicated?"

"It means you have been identified as having knowledge of a crime."

"I know what it means. Do I need a lawyer?"

"That is for you to decide. Usually, innocent people do not need an attorney."

"Ask your questions."

"About your pain trial, without naming names or correlating names to numbers, what is the percentage of success resulting from your revised pain regime? What is success for your trial?"

"Why is that relevant to your investigation?"

"The answer to that will become obvious soon."

"Fifty, maybe fifty-two percent, of the patients benefit from the revised regime."

"I see. About half experience less pain. Is that correct?'

"Close enough."

"Does the percentage hold for all types of cancer?"

Greene squirms, looks down, steels herself, and then unblinkingly answers the detective's question.

"No."

"I see. Some cancers benefit from the pain cocktail, and some do not."

"No, you don't *see*, Detective. Your use of the word *cocktail* is pejorative, and I don't approve. In my trial, we use an approved mix of pain medications. Do you know what it is like to have a decade of work — to have your life's mission go down the drain? You do not know what it is like to spend eighteen-hour days searching, hoping, and begging for the epiphany to stop the suffering. No, Detective Trimble, you don't understand. Your mother understood the pain. That is why she kept her suffering from you."

Greene mentioning her mother triggers the beginning of an episode. Not wanting a repeat from yesterday or last night's dream, Carin falls on her training and PTSD counseling sessions to remain focused and in the moment.

"I don't comprehend how difficult it must be for people living with cancer. One day, I hope you and I can chat and help me grasp the depth of the suffering. Today, however, we have concerns about our investigation. Why did you support murder?"

"Support murder? What are you talking about?"

"Dr. Greene, Sharon, we have been given information you were aware of who committed the murders and did nothing to report your knowledge."

"That is speculative."

"Yes."

"And?"

"And why didn't you do anything when you knew your patients were being killed?" Carin is enjoying the quick exchange.

"First, is that thing on?"

Mojtabai interjects.

"For the record, Dr. Greene is indicating the recording device. Yes, as stated at the beginning of the session, we are recording the video and audio with a timestamp."

"Thank you. I didn't say anything because I knew."

"What did you know?" Carin raises her spine. Her attention is focused solely on the doctor.

"I knew I was being framed."

"Framed? By whom?"

"The murderer, who else?"

"Sorry. Who do you think was trying to frame you by killing your patients?" Carin's eyes squint.

"Jared McKinnon."

Dr. Greene and Deena Demchuk are sent home with orders to return to resume the interviews the following afternoon. The interview sessions have been exhausting. When he calls it a day, Trimble and Mojtabai are in hour four of a review.

Using her techniques, Carin was able to prevent the dream from recurring. She enjoys her fancy new microwave. There are buttons for several automated cooking options. After experimenting, the Popcorn button is the right time and power setting to cook the prepackaged breakfast sausage biscuit, giving her enough time to brush her hair.

Happy with the information they have gathered, Carin plans to arrive at the office before six. The early arrival will give her enough time to prepare for the review with Mojtabai.

"What time did you get here?"

"Good morning to you, too, Detective Carin."

"Sorry. Good morning, Mosh. You're early."

"I got here about five-thirty. We have a lot to cover.

Five hours and too many cups of coffee into the review, Carin is wavering.

"Let's go over it again." Mojtabai is not satisfied with their lack of conclusions.

"Mosh, we have been over it six times. Greene thinks McKinnon needed the money and used her patients as his funding source."

"It is easy to blame the dead guy. Carin, why would Greene think she was being framed?"

"She says framed. I think she uses framed when she means exposed. Maybe she means framed *and* exposed. What did McKinnon say in his letter to Al? Something like '*Don't let the actions of one doctor...*' Greene claimed the trial's funding was drying up. More negative exposure would mean the end of her experiment."

"Let's run with that — for thirty minutes, then some lunch. Greene and Demchuk will be here at 1:30."

"Agreed."

*** *** ***

"Do you own stock in this café?" Mojtabai's tone is bright, and his smile lightens Carin's mood.

"Funny. If you haven't noticed, there are not a lot of decent places to eat. I've eaten enough meat and potatoes to last a lifetime. Also, winters are tough here. It is nice to sit in the sun."

Carin stops talking and looks over Mojtabai's shoulder. Looking back, the agent sees Laura approaching.

"Hello, Laura." Carin used a bright voice when Laura

was close enough.

Laura puts her hand to the side of her head, between her forehead and ear, and then waves her palm outward. She repeats the hello for Mojtabai, turns back to Carin, and points to her phone. Carin understands and opens the text app on her phone — placing it so Mojtabai can also read Laura's texts.

> **Laura-Mara**
> *Al knows.*

"What does Al know?"

> **Laura-Mara**
> *Al knows who killed those people.*

"How do you know that Al knows who committed the murders?"

> **Laura-Mara**
> *He told me.*

"What did Al say, exactly?"

> **Laura-Mara**
> *He knows who killed those people. He can't tell us.*

"Did he say why he is keeping it a secret?"

Laura-Mara
No place to live.

"No place to live — I don't understand."

Laura-Mara
You need to check on Al.

"Do you think Al is in trouble?"

Laura-Mara
*I don't know. He has not texted me
since yesterday.*

"Laura, thank you for the information. We'll go right now and check on Al."

Laura-Mara
Don't let anything bad happen to Al.

"I won't let anything bad happen to Al."

* * *
** ** **

Admiring the pristine lawn, Carin leads Mojtabai onto the Demchuk porch and the front door. Al answers the doorbell, opens the screen door, and waves, requesting the duo enter. Carin notices Al looks like he has not cleaned up in a few days. Silently, Al shows the agent and the detective to the den. In the bed, opposite an elaborate model train setup, John Demchuk lies on his back, staring at the ceiling. The ice pick sticking out of his chest has created a ring of red in the duvet. Carin steps into the room, close to Al, and Mojtabai steps out to make the 911 call from the hallway.

"Do you know what happened?"

Al doesn't answer. Fearing he killed his father, Carin leans in and discovers John Demchuk is breathing.

"Mosh! We need an ambulance — he's still alive."

* * *
** **

Carin returns from the den to the hallway and Mojtabai.

"Mari says she thinks there is one puncture to the heart. Because the attacker left the pick in the heart, Demchuk survived. He didn't bleed out. Mosh, why didn't he fight? It looks like he laid there and let someone stab him."

"Carin, I don't know. Maybe John was drugged or simply asleep. Do you think Al did this?"

"I don't know. We'll delay the interviews. We need to know more about John Demchuk. Where is Al?"

They find Al seated at the breakfast table, and Mosh lets Carin talk to her friend.

"Al, you like it here, in the breakfast nook."

"Yes."

"Your mother will be home soon. I called and canceled the meeting. Are you okay?" Mojtabai watches as Carin's soft voice pushes the pain away from Al's face.

"Can I stay with you?"

"Why do you want to stay with me?"

"Not safe here."

Carin and Mojtabai exchange a look of confusion.

"Partner, you can't stay with me. We will get you a room where you will be safe." Carin is desperate to ease Al's fragile emotions.

"A hotel?"

"Yes."

"Will they have porridge?"

"Yes, they will have oatmeal in the morning. It will only be a few days. Then you can come home. Is that okay?

"A few days."

"Partner, your father will be okay. Can you tell me why it is not safe here?"

"A few days, then it will be safe."

"How do you know it will be safe in a few days? Help me understand."

"Laura is my friend."

Carin knows Al is somewhere else, and pressing him now for questions is unlikely to be beneficial.

Carin and Mosh were in the conference room for a few hours when the door opened unexpectedly, with Jan Kolston stepping into the room.

"Detective Trimble, Agent Mojtabai, good morning."

"Good morning? It's nearly noon." Carin is too literal for Mosh's liking.

"Good *morning*, Jan. What's up?"

"Carin, Deena Demchuk calls once an hour demanding to know where her son Al is being hidden. It's kind of annoying."

Mosh goes into his PC, which is his way of silently telling Carin to deal with Jan's Deena problem.

"Jan, I'm surprised you're asking for help."

"I don't need help. I need permission. Detective Newbie."

Carin accepts the good-natured ribbing.

"Ha. Did Deena tell you where she is?"

"No."

"Okay. Detective Know-Nothing says you can arrest Deena Demchuk if she decides to show up. Arrest her after a final warning if she does not stop harassing the department."

Jan leaves with a sly grin.

"Mosh, anything from forensics?"

"Funny you ask. Advanced DNA techniques are pretty cool. Even the team way out here in the middle of nowhere can run a sequence in a few hours. Deena Demchuk's DNA is on the ice pick, but —"

"Al can't be excluded." Carin's volume fades into the air.

"Correct. Who stabbed John Demchuk?" Mosh is determined to get Carin to stay focused.

"My guess is Deena."

"Why?"

"Because John kept her from living the life he promised. The life she thinks she deserves."

"And?"

Leaning back, thinking, Carin surprises herself when she speaks.

"Because John knows everything."

"Agreed. What does John know? Why did Deena stab her husband?"

"To hide the truth."

"What truth?" Carin turns mute at her quick response.

"Detective, you have been avoiding the reality. Take your emotions out of the equation. What truth?"

Carin sucks a deep, long breath, exhales, and responds.

"Al killed those people."

"Except for the nail polish and the ring, that is what the evidence says. And?"

"Maybe Deena went to the nursing home to try and create a cover story for her son. Al killed McKinnon because he caught his mother bumping uglies with McKinnon."

"Is Al capable of making it look like a suicide?"

"No. I meant McKinnon shot himself because he disappointed, well, everyone. Al was the straw that broke his mind."

Chapter Twenty-Two

"For the record, I am Special Agent Karim Mojtabai. Detective Carin Trimble and Deena Clarin Demchuk are with me. Mr. Boudreaux Thibodeaux is present to represent Mrs. Demchuk."

"Thank you all for agreeing to meet. Mrs. Demchuk, we have quite a few questions. Is there anything you'd like to say before we begin?"

"I didn't kill anyone."

"Deena, I told you to be quiet. Special Agent, my client reserves all rights under the Fifth Amendment."

Thibodeaux's molasses-sweet southern drawl is easy on the ears. Mojtabai continues with his professional voice.

"Mr. Thibodeaux."

"Call me Tib."

"Tib, we have your client's DNA on the weapon."

"Of course you do. Mrs. Demchuk lives in the house and has used the implement countless times."

"Also, based on the DNA profile, we could not exclude your client's son, Marcus Alvin Demchuk."

"Al didn't do anything. You and Detective Know-Nothing are shit-for-brains clueless." Deena went off — surprising no one. Tib raises a finger to be heard.

"Mrs. Demchuk, quit being ugly and hush your mouth. I am going to say this one more time. You had to hire me because of your inappropriate relationship with your prior attorney. I agreed to represent you, and you agreed to listen and adhere to my advice. You will remain silent unless I agree the question is something you should and can answer. Do you understand?"

"Yes."

"Mrs. Demchuk, we can place you in Tercia LeClare's room." Carin smiles internally. The session is progressing according to the plan she and Mojtabai discussed.

"Detective, hold your horses. That is speculation." Tib is firm and clear.

"A grand jury will decide how speculative it is."

"Are you charging my client?"

"Not at this time. We have additional interviews to conduct before we go to the grand jury."

"A grand jury usually implies a conspiracy or multiple defendants." Tib knows the law.

"Multiple defendants?" Deena is lost and frustrated.

"I told you to stay quiet. Let me handle this."

"No! Tib. No. I want to know who they think is involved. Tell me."

Mojtabai turns his chair and leans over. Carin mirrors the agent's movement. Nearly face-to-face with their elbows on their knees, Mojtabai silently moves his mouth. It is a diversion. Deena and Tib cannot see the wink Mojtabai gives Carin. Sitting tall, Carin continues with the plan.

"Mrs. Demchuk, your son Al, along with Dr. Greene, are persons of interest in the recent murders."

"What do you mean, Al? Al had nothing to do with anything."

"Deena, stop talking."

"No, Tib. I want a deal."

Mojtabai leans in, places his palms on the table, and speaks.

"For the record, Mrs. Demchuk has requested a deal in exchange for information. Unfortunately, the attack on John Demchuk is not being considered for a reduced sentence."

Tib Thibodeaux is an experienced criminal defense attorney. He sniffs, reclines, and oozes his Southern charm.

"Not the attack on John. We may have information regarding the Nursing Home Murders. A deal, Mojtabai — all or none."

"All of what?"

"Probation for everything my client knows about who committed the Nursing Home Murders, the Jared McKinnon death — both McKinnons — and the John Demchuk attack."

Carin and Mojtabai realize instantly that Thibodeaux came to the interview ready to cut a deal. Also, the death of the senior McKinnon was ruled a heart attack, not murder. Carin immediately decides the new information is both good and bad. Mojtabai closes the session and presses the intercom for the duty sergeant.

"Sergeant Kolston."

"Kolston, a deputy to escort Mrs. Demchuk, please."

"She's on her way."

Mojtabai makes the request of his partner.

"Detective Trimble, if you please."

"Deena Clarin Demchuk, you are under arrest for the

attack on your husband, John Alvin Demchuk."

"Tib, you said no jail."

"Don't worry. We'll have you bonded out in an hour."

"Out? I don't want to be in!"

Carin looks to Thibodaux, who raises his eyebrows in response, allowing Carin to ask.

"Deena, what do you want?"

"No death penalty."

"We don't have the death penalty in this state. Attempted murder can be anywhere from ten years to life. Is what you are going to tell us that serious?"

"I want to know Al will be safe."

"You have my word. No harm will come to Al."

"You keep him away from that Laura girl."

Stunned, Carin realizes Deena is jealous of her son's relationship with a woman. The female deputy steps into the room and stands with her back to the wall, waiting. Carin puts up a hand, requesting the deputy to remain before she continues to question the suspect.

"I will not keep Al from being happy. Deena, what are you trying to say?"

"Take the Fifth. You don't have the deal yet. Close your yap, and let me get you what we discussed." Tib knows he is fighting a losing battle with his client.

"Enough." Deena is giving up. Carin seizes the moment and uses her training to turn up her persuasive skills.

"Deena, why did you do it?"

"Sharon."

"What about Dr. Greene?"

"She lied."

"What did Dr. Greene lie about?"

"The pain. My mother died in pain. Before Sharon started that so-called trial, nothing worked, and *The Doctor* kept saying, *'We'll try this next.'* She's a lying bitch. All doctors are liars."

"I think I am beginning to understand. You wanted to punish Dr. Greene for not helping your mother's pain. Correct?" Carin's tone of voice captured Deena's attention.

"Yes."

"I see. What about Jared McKinnon? You mentioned him earlier."

"Jared comforted me when my mother passed. Jared knew I was seeing his father. When his father died, Jared and I grew closer."

"Do you know how the senior McKinnon died?"

"Yes."

"Can you tell me what you know about Jared McKinnon Senior's death?"

Shuffling in her seat at the pained memory, Deena Demchuk spits the truth in a staccato string of words.

"Jared Senior died of a heart attack while we were having sex in the storeroom."

"That must have been traumatic for you."

"Pushing him off me, off the table, and onto the floor was traumatic. Pulling up his pants before calling for help was upsetting."

Pushing the imagery out of her head, Carin presses forward with her inquiry.

"What do you know about Jared Junior's death?"

"That wimp shot himself."

Deena departs into a silent memory. Carin concludes that Jared McKinnon Junior's love for Deena Demchuk might have been one-sided. The accused resumes her clipped summary, forcing Carin to focus.

"We had just finished. Jared always finished quickly. I was getting dressed when Jared pulled the gun from the nightstand and sat on the bed."

"Why did he kill himself?"

"Because I told him he was my fuck-buddy. You don't marry your fuck-buddy."

"I am a little confused. Why did you continue the affair if you thought Jared was a wimp and not someone you would consider husband material?"

"Did you see how he was hung?"

Ignoring the imagery and the continued emergence of Deena's true personality, Carin follows up with a new line of questions.

"Let's move to John, your husband."

"John the Limp Wimp. Even when he took the pills, he didn't know what to do with it."

"Why did you stab your husband?"

"Because Al told John what I did."

"May I have a moment with my client?"

"No, Tib. I told you already. Enough is enough. They know the truth. What they don't know is why."

Carin accepts Thibodeaux's wave of dismissal toward his client as permission to continue with her questions.

"What did Al tell your husband about what you did?"

"Al figured out it was me. Months ago, hell, over a year ago, Al knew."

"How did Al know?"

"I don't know. At least, I am not sure."

Deena goes silent and into her head, searching for a memory.

* * *

In the McKinnon residence's main bedroom, a few weeks after his father's death, Deena is forcing her new and willing lover, Jared Junior, to do things people regret in the morning.

"*Come on, Jared, tell me how it could be done.*"

"*I told you, no. Slide over. Move up. Your knees are hurting my arms.*"

"*No, not until you tell me.*"

"*Stop that! You'll stain the sheets.*"

"*I've got more. Tell me.*"

"*Okay. If you want to kill someone with no trace or murder weapon, explode the heart.*"

"*How do you do that?*"

"*Stop! I'll have to throw these sheets away and get a new mattress. Stop!*"

"*Tell me.*"

"*You are close, aren't you? Deena, how close?*"

"*Yes, I am close to a big one. Tell me.*"

"*Put a huge air bubble in an I-V and let it travel to the*" *heart. It is almost impossible to kill someone using the bubble process. The air bubble is too large to insert and cause death effectively."*

Deena continues to grind her knees on Jared's biceps, her pelvis on his chin.

"How else?"

"Stick a needle in the pericardium lining and either collapse or explode the heart."

Deena reaches her goal and rolls off of her lover.

** ** **

Carin pulls Deena out of her head and back into the now.

"Mrs. Demchuk, you claimed you don't know how Al learned about your activities. Is there anything you can think of that might indicate how your son learned the details of your double life?"

"Jared told me to stick a needle in the pericardium lining and destroy the heart. He must have told Al what I knew."

"Did Jared McKinnon aid you in the murders?"

"Detective, hold up. Deena, this was not what we discussed. Stop talking, and let me get you a deal."

"Tib, it doesn't matter anymore, does it?"

Shaking his head signifies a reluctant acceptance of his client's choice. Tib allows Carin to resume when he closes the cover on his notes.

"Deena, did Jared McKinnon aid you in the murders?"

"Are you kidding? Jared barfed when I mashed a frog by mistake. You'd think a mortician, a certified pathologist, would not be squeamish. Jared put it together. He was another wimp who was not strong enough to do anything."

Surprising Carin, Mojtabai ends the session.

"That is enough for today. The deputy will escort you to a holding cell. Mister Thibodeaux, write up your offer. We'll review it and take it to the district attorney."

Rising to leave, Deena pleads with her eyes and voice.

"Carin, will you make sure Al is okay?"

"Yes, Deena, I will make sure Al is okay."

** ** **

"Come on, Louie, stop worrying. They solved the murders. You can relax. That woman wanted revenge on Dr. Greene. The news says she was leading a double life. It has nothing to do with you."

"It has everything to do with me. You don't understand."

"Then help me understand. I can't help you if you don't tell me what is bugging you."

She pulls on her favorite T-shirt, one discarded by Kel. It is just long enough to reach her thighs. The blue shirt matches her cobalt blue panties. She chose the shirt because she knows her man likes blue. Louie props the pillows and climbs under the sheets before giving Kel her story.

"The news report indicated the killer used a needle to murder people who were days or weeks from dying. Most of the victims went to the McKinnon Funeral Home. You know how the news reported Deena Demchuk conspired with Jared McKinnon?"

"The news claimed McKinnon and Demchuk conspired. What about it?" Confused by the details his wife is bringing up, Kel waits. Louie takes a moment before admitting what she suspects.

"I don't think McKinnon helped Deena. I think he knew what Deena was doing and accepted the money when the bodies came to him for processing. Maybe. I don't know. I'm tired."

Slinking down, pulling the comforter to her chin, and checking that Booger is snoring in the corner, Louie tries to end the discussion.

"Kel, it's nothing. It's just."

"Just what?"

"Clinic security wants to talk to Sharon and me tomorrow. Not just us. I think everyone who has access to the dispensers is being interviewed."

"Do you know why?"

"I'm not sure. There is talk of missing drugs. That can't be right. The dispensers have video monitoring and two-factor access controls. Something else is happening."

Rolling away, trying to end the conversation, Louie knows Kel will persist until she tells her husband what she knows.

"Spit it out."

"A few months ago, I saw pericardial needle kits in the pocket of Sharon's lab coat."

Epilogue

On a rainy Saturday morning, two weeks after the Deena Demchuk confession, Carin opts to skip zapping a frozen breakfast sausage muffin in favor of the cozy café. The rain forced her inside. Luckily, the early hour meant one of the tables near a window was available. Spied by Mari on her daily morning run, Carin is pleased when the wet and sweaty EMT steps into the café.

Carin coyly watches Mari shake off the drizzle and order. Happily for Carin, Mari sits at her table. The EMT slides across a fresh black coffee to match her own. Mari accepts Carin's meek thank-you nod. The nervous detective pushes her empty plate, with the empty coffee mug, to the side before picking up the fresh coffee and giving a wink of thanks to her new friend.

"Good morning. I run by here every morning — I've not seen you here this early."

"You've seen me here?" Despite her rural childhood on the farm, Carin doesn't think she will ever get used to living in a small town.

"Carin, you probably eat lunch here three times a week. It is a small town, and you like that chair on the sidewalk next to this window."

"Are you stalking me?" A smile takes the unintended bite out of Carin's question.

"No. You know, I drive a lot of miles? It is called Main Street for a reason."

"Fair enough and good morning. How are you?"

"I am good. What is that you are eating?"

"This is something Melba makes for me. It's a sausage biscuit with no butter, cheese, or sauce. Well, no added butter. Just a buttermilk biscuit and breakfast sausage. I like the protein and the carbs to start my day. Plus, buttermilk biscuits are tasty."

"Melba makes you a special breakfast?"

"She got tired of seeing me drink coffee for breakfast and insisted I tell her what I liked to eat in the morning."

"Marble Grove is a small town with friendly people. Paradise." Mari's light comment forces Carin to accept reality.

"Yes, it is nice here."

"Is that why you stay?"

A little stunned at the direct question from someone who is becoming her friend, someone whom she hardly knows, Carin leans back and answers.

"I could go anywhere. Marble Grove is nice enough. The pay is okay. The people are kind. Maybe I'll find someone here."

Mari's grin at the inference is upbeat.

"Carin, what do you know about Robert LeClare?"

"Robert LeClare? Nothing. Why?"

"Our former dispatcher has lived in Hemingway County for all her sixty-seven years." Confused by Mari's non-sequitur, Carin asks simply.

"Dispatcher?"

"Emmaline Zumbro, the policeman's grandmother. She has been working for the county for fifty years, almost all in dispatch. First for the police department, then the fire department. Our org, the EMTs, roll up to the fire chief."

"I don't know Emmaline. Should I?"

"I am surprised you don't yet know Emmaline. It wouldn't hurt for you to know her. Call her Emmy, and she knows everything and everyone. A person like Emmy is always a good person to know."

"Let me guess. Emmy likes to talk."

After a quick giggle, Mari's cheeks, still rosy from the run, tell the story.

"She can talk and then some. Did you know Marble Grove has never had a real crime problem? Well, not until the murders."

"I believe it. Lots of small towns see almost no serious crime."

"Do you know why Marble Grove avoided crime when the town was broke? This place almost went bankrupt and still never experienced a serious crime problem."

Carin finds and presses crumbs together before downing the last of the tasty biscuit, sips coffee that's too hot, and then waits for Mari to continue.

"Marble Grove had one drug dealer for more than two decades. You went to one person if you wanted illegal drugs or a hooker. There was one place to go if you wanted to sell something with questionable ownership rights."

"Robert LeClare?" Carin is becoming suspicious.

"Robert LeClare."

"Why are you telling me this?"

"I don't think all the murders were altruistic revenge."

Stone-faced and unmoving, Carin assesses Mari's comment and waits.

"You are good. Is it a detective thing to sit silently, knowing the interviewee or the criminal will always want to talk?"

"Something like that. You are not a criminal, are you?"

"Not today." Mari's cheeks rise in a grin as she raises her coffee mug.

"Why do you think some murders were not altruistic revenge?" Locking eyes, Carin waits. Mari sips coffee just cool enough not to burn, then answers Carin's question.

"A better way to phrase it might be: Not all the murders were altruistic. Most of the victims would have been dead in a few days. Why kill someone who is knocking on death's door?"

"Revenge."

Mari is practically glowing and happy to continue.

"Exactly. Why does someone want revenge? Love? Maybe. Money? Possibly. Anger? Definitely. Anger for what? For being hurt."

"Hurt?" The raised eyebrow is intentional.

"Hurt by being made to do things you regret."

Carin's cheeks match Mari's rosy color — an unspoken bond is growing between the women.

"What did Deena regret?"

Mari's question feels rhetorical to the detective.

"You tell me."

Before Mari can answer, the women are interrupted.

"Hello, ladies. May I join you?"

Without waiting for permission, Marg Lyttle pulls a chair close enough to join Carin and Mari as the third at a table sized for two.

"Hello. Marg, right?"

"Yes, Detective. Good memory."

"Call me Carin. This is Mari."

"I know who Mari is — how's your mother?"

"Mom is good. Thanks."

Marg smiles too broadly to be comfortable as she turns from Mari to Carin.

"Detective Carin, have you searched Tercia LeClare's house yet?"

"Why would I search Tercia LeClare's house?"

"It's more of an apartment — one of those duplex things, like where I live, only smaller. Anyway. Deena Demchuk used to live in the other half of the LeClare duplex. The one down the end of Mayberry Street, past the high school."

"LeClare duplex?"

"I am surprised you don't know. Robert LeClare owned several rental properties."

Ignoring Marg's "Minnesota Nice" barb, Carin keeps an even tone.

"I see. Why would I want to search Tercia's apartment?"

"Because that's where the clues are, silly."

Annoyed at the busybody's bubbly tone intended to stick a thorn in her side, Carin holds her comments and reluctantly decides to ask politely.

"Clues to what, exactly?"

"The murders, of course. You don't think Deena did all that alone, do you? Oh, look at the time. I have to run. Toodle Doodle."

Carin and Mari watch Marg push the chair back to where she got it. She says a too-loud goodbye to Melba, then exits with a bounce in her step. When the ringing of the tiny bell on the door ends, Mari has a question for her newest friend.

"What are you going to do?"

Carin spots a bird landing in one of the young elm trees that dot the sidewalks of Main Street. Knowing the city has committed to keeping the hybridized trees alive gives Carin a warm feeling about Marble Grove and her future.

"Look, there. That is a Loggerhead Shrike. It is rare to see one here. Minnesota is part of their breeding grounds."

"Your friend Al has rubbed off on you."

"Yes, I suppose he has. I have always enjoyed nature and birds. I have learned and now understand Al's joy in knowing the birds."

Carin watches until the bird flies away before turning to Mari. She is unblinking and wondering if she can discuss the next step. Professionalism takes over, and Carin responds with the truth.

"On Monday, I am going to look into Robert and Tercia LeClare. Maybe there is something there — maybe not. A married couple with lots of history should be interesting."

"They were not married. They were twins. You'd never know it. They are so different. I met them when I was little.

Tercia was a tiny thing with blonde hair. Robert Jr. was called Bobby. He had dark hair like his father's, and he was thick. Not fat, just big. Looking into their history and what they did for Marble Grove is a good idea. Also, check in with Marc."

"The coroner, Marc?"

"Yes, that Marc."

"Why?" Carin's tone turned sharp because she doesn't like being given hints without context.

"He completed his forensic fellowship, and he passed the board. Marc is a certified forensic pathologist. I am surprised you didn't know."

"I didn't know." Carin's meek response is acceptance of another Minnesota Nice verbal barb. Pausing to enjoy the moment and the company, Carin is surprised by her internal dialogue leaking out.

"Do you know more? Mari, what can you tell me?"

"I know a lot more that is secondhand hearsay. You need to find facts."

"Understood. Secondhand and hearsay are redundant." Realizing her mother's training has escaped, Carin tries to make amends.

"Sorry, that was rude. Any information could hold clues and help me find the correct search path."

Mari grins again and ignores her new friend's pedantic nature.

"Carin, let's go for a run. I'll meet you at your place tomorrow morning at five."

Stunned at Mari's abrupt change in tone and posture,

Carin agrees.

"I'd like that. Running helps the PTSD. Five a.m."

Thank you!

"'THANK YOU' IS THE BEST PRAYER THAT ANYONE COULD SAY. I SAY THAT ONE A LOT. THANK YOU EXPRESSES EXTREME GRATITUDE, HUMILITY, UNDERSTANDING."
— ALICE WALKER

Please accept my gratitude for spending your precious time reading my story. I am often reminded of how lucky I am to write and do more than I ever imagined.

"WHEN I STARTED COUNTING MY BLESSINGS, MY WHOLE LIFE TURNED AROUND."
— WILLIE NELSON

I have my health, a loving family, a wonderful wife, and an overwhelming yearning to keep them all.

R. C.

P.S. Don't forget to leave a review!

About R. C.

Two people sparked my interest in reading in secondary school (high school for Americans): a close friend and an instructor. The instructor took an interest in the education of a boy he once called "The rebel without a clue." He helped me to learn the value of an enjoyable book.

The instructor required me to read exciting historical novels for academic credit. Frank Norris, Leon Uris, and Ken Follett inspire and fuel my love of history. My lifelong friend encouraged me to read Frank Herbert and J. R. R. Tolkien. I became addicted to science/fantasy.

I was born into a military family. Following the military tradition was logical. However, after years of "yes, sirs" and scraping the wax off floors, I decided there must be more fun in a corporate career.

After forty-plus years of work experience across the globe, I landed in Minnesota.

Works by R. C.

Science Fiction
The Carina Reality
Cold Star

Terran Star

Affinity Star

Time Star

Calm Star

Hearth Star

Bairn Star

Five Evils Star

Reluctant Star

Light Star

Second Star

Gossamer Star

The Kathla Chronicles
Threshold

Mysteries & Thrillers
Tule Fog

Max and the Dream Time

Miranda Everlasting

Aydin Trammell Chronicles
Shiny Lies

Shiny Pennies

Carin Trimble Mysteries
Marble Grove
Calder Road
Broken Loch

Other Writings
Crazy Sweet Grass
Fourth Street Blues
Vampire Unicorn

You can find links to my books or contact me through my website and socials.

My Website:
www.rcducantlin.com

Facebook
www.facebook.com/rcducantlin

Twitter
www.twitter.com/rcducantlin

LinkedIn
www.linkedin.com/in/rcducantlin

Made in the USA
Middletown, DE
02 June 2024

55186430R00159